Join the Little House Family
Five Generations of Pioneer Girls

Martha Morse, Laura's great-grandmother
born 1782

Martha was born to a wealthy landowning family in Scotland. She loved her family, but she also wanted to see the world, and one day she left her home to start a new life in America.

Charlotte Tucker, Laura's grandmother
born 1809

Martha's daughter Charlotte was born a city girl, and grew up near the bustling port of Boston. Charlotte had a restless spirit and traveled farther and farther west, before settling in Wisconsin.

Caroline Quiner, Laura's mother
born 1839

Charlotte's daughter Caroline spent her childhood in Wisconsin, and her days were busy helping her mother keep their little frontier farm running. Caroline grew up to be Ma Ingalls, Laura's mother.

Laura Ingalls
born 1867

Caroline's daughter Laura traveled by covered wagon across the frontier. When Laura grew up, she realized the ways of the pioneer were ending and wrote down the stories of her childhood in the Little House books.

Rose Wilder, Laura's daughter
born 1886

Laura's daughter, Rose, traveled from South Dakota to the Ozark Mountains of Missouri. She grew up hearing the stories of her mother's frontier girlhood and determined that one day she would be a new kind of pioneer.

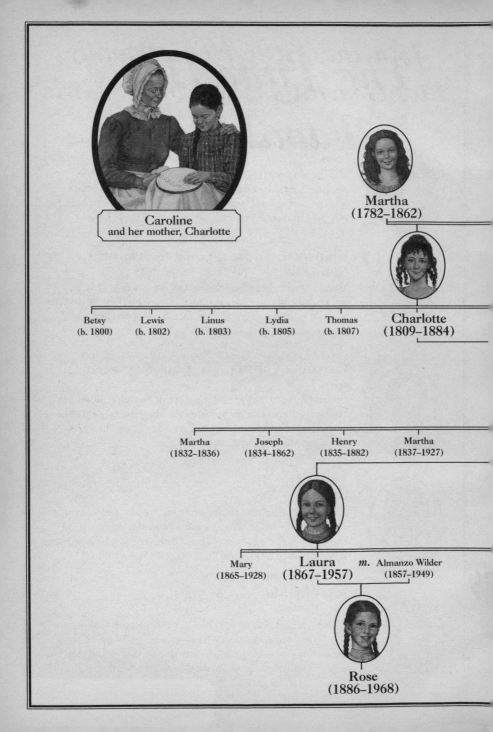

Caroline
and her mother, Charlotte

Martha
(1782–1862)

Charlotte
(1809–1884)

Betsy
(b. 1800)

Lewis
(b. 1802)

Linus
(b. 1803)

Lydia
(b. 1805)

Thomas
(b. 1807)

Martha
(1832–1836)

Joseph
(1834–1862)

Henry
(1835–1882)

Martha
(1837–1927)

Mary
(1865–1928)

Laura
(1867–1957)

m. Almanzo Wilder
(1857–1949)

Rose
(1886–1968)

The Little House
Family Tree

m.   Lewis Tucker

m.   Henry Quiner   Caroline   Mary   Nancy   George
       (1807–1844)   (b. 1811)   (b. 1813)   (b. 1816)   (1820–1821)

Caroline   *m.*   Charles Ingalls   Eliza   Thomas
(1839–1924)   (1836–1902)   (1842–1931)   (1844–1903)

Caroline   Charles   Grace
(1870–1946)   (1875–1876)   (1877–1941)

Little House *in* Brookfield

Maria D. Wilkes

Illustrations by Dan Andreasen

SCHOLASTIC INC.
New York Toronto London Auckland Sydney
Mexico City New Delhi Hong Kong

ISBN 0-439-10502-1

Text copyright © 1996 by HarperCollins Publishers Inc.
Illustrations copyright © 1996 by Dan Andreasen.
All rights reserved. Published by Scholastic Inc.,
555 Broadway, New York, NY 10012, by arrangement
with HarperCollins Children's Books, a division of
HarperCollins Publishers. Little House® and The Caroline Years™ are
trademarks of HarperCollins Publishers Inc. SCHOLASTIC and associated
logos are trademarks and/or registered trademarks of Scholastic Inc.

12 11 10 9 8 7 6 5 4 3   0 1 2 3 4/0

Printed in the U.S.A.   40

First Scholastic printing, August 1999

Typography by Alicia Mikles

To Peter,
who makes the thoughts clearer,
the words truer,
the moments richer

Author's Note

Before Laura Ingalls Wilder ever penned the Little House books, she wrote to her aunt Martha Quiner Carpenter, asking her to "tell the story of those days" when she and Laura's mother, Caroline, were growing up in Brookfield, Wisconsin. Aunt Martha sent Laura a series of letters that were filled with family reminiscences and vividly described the Quiners' life back in the 1800's. These letters have served as the basis for LITTLE HOUSE IN BROOKFIELD, *the first in a series of stories about Caroline Quiner, who married Charles Ingalls and became Laura's beloved Ma.*

The Caroline Quiner Ingalls whom I've come to know through Aunt Martha's letters, personal accounts, and my own research is, I was surprised and delighted to discover, even more animated, engaging, and outspoken than the fictional Caroline that millions of readers have grown to know and love. I have presented the most realistic account possible of Caroline Quiner's life in LITTLE HOUSE IN BROOKFIELD, *while still remaining true to the familiar depiction of Ma in the Little House books. I would like to thank everyone who contributed historical and biographical information and support and who directed me toward significant original sources, diaries, and documents, especially William Anderson, Martin Sandler, the late Roger Lea MacBride, Abigail MacBride, Noel Silverman, and Martin Perkins, Curator of Research and Interpretation, The State Historical Society of Wisconsin.*

—M.D.W.

Contents

Little House
in
Brookfield

Hotcakes and Sugar Syrup

Caroline blinked and rubbed her eyes. Wiggling her toes under the sheet, she stretched her arms above her head as high as she could.

"Caroline!" Three-year-old Eliza tugged on Caroline's sleeve. Caroline put her finger to her lips. "Hush!" she whispered, as Eliza's bright eyes sparkled up at her. "You'll wake Martha!"

Martha, sound asleep on the other side of Eliza, had the linen sheet pulled right up to her chin. Martha was the oldest sister. She was eight years old, and she didn't like it when Caroline or Eliza woke her up.

Hazy shafts of light began spilling through the window as the rising sun awakened the dark, sleepy sky. Caroline sat up and wriggled her way to the foot of the bed. She peeked around the curtain that separated the two beds in the room. The sheet on the boys' bed still covered two big lumps. Her brothers, Joseph and Henry, were not yet awake.

But Mother was. Her brisk footsteps echoed back and forth over the wooden floor in the kitchen below. Caroline could hear fat pork sizzling in the frying pan, and she knew the sweet smell of hotcakes would soon fill the whole house.

Mother's footsteps were loud and firm as she climbed the stairs to the children's room. Her straight black hair was neatly pinned behind her head, and her green eyes already looked tired. "Good morning, Caroline and Eliza," Mother said as she peered through the stair railing.

Every morning, Mother looked at the girls' bed first, expecting to find Caroline awake and ready to help her start the day. Caroline loved helping Mother and making her smile. Especially now, when Mother didn't smile nearly as much as she used to.

"Good morning," Caroline replied softly.

"Time to wake Martha and the boys, Caroline. The sun's already rising, and the morning's wasting. Hurry, now." As quickly as she had appeared, Mother disappeared down the stairs.

Caroline reached over Eliza and gently shook Martha's arm. "Mother says to wake up, Martha."

Martha pulled the sheet over her head and grumbled, "Hush, Caroline. It's time to sleep."

"Up, Martha, up!" Eliza sang, bouncing up and down.

Caroline slid out of bed. A cool early-morning draft floated above the wooden boards, chilling her bare feet. Lifting the hem of her cotton nightgown off the floor, she pushed the curtain aside and tiptoed over to the boys' bed. Gently she shook Henry, who was still asleep.

Henry pushed the sandy curls away from his face and sat up, startled. "Morning already, little Brownbraid?" he asked. His blue eyes were still full of sleep.

Ever since she was three years old, Caroline had been called "little Brownbraid." One morning when they had still lived in a log cabin instead of their big frame house, Mother had twisted Caroline's thick, soft hair into a long brown braid. Father noticed it at breakfast and said, "How pretty you are, little Brownbraid!" and that became his special name for her. "How's my little Brownbraid?" he'd say, and tug lightly on the bottom of her braid.

Caroline missed Father. He had been gone for almost one whole year. Soon after all the leaves had fallen from the trees, he had sailed away on a big boat called a schooner, and he had never come back. Mother said Father was in heaven. Caroline missed him tugging on her braid. She wondered if his schooner was in heaven, too.

"Mother says it's time to get up," Caroline said importantly.

"Then it must be time to get up!"

Henry nudged Joseph as Caroline turned back to the girls' bed and pulled the curtain behind her. As she lifted Eliza from under the covers, Caroline heard her brothers jump out of their bed and pull their trousers and shirts on. The floorboards creaked and shook as they thundered barefoot down the stairs.

All of a sudden, the room began to smell like Mother's hotcakes, and Caroline was in a hurry. She shook Martha's arm once more. "Wake up!"

Martha threw the quilt back and leaned up on her elbows. "All right, all right," she yawned. "I'm awake."

Reaching into the middle drawer of the tall chest that stood at the foot of their bed, Caroline pulled out her everyday dress and white petticoat and set them neatly on the mattress. She opened the bottom drawer and took out Eliza's dress and petticoat. Eliza squirmed out of her nightgown, and Caroline whisked her into her clothes. After dressing herself, Caroline turned her back to Martha and waited impatiently as Martha sleepily fastened the long row of buttons on the back of her blue cotton dress.

"Hurry, Martha," Caroline urged.

"It's too early to hurry." Martha yawned as she finished buttoning Caroline's dress.

Caroline didn't think it was too early. She was too busy thinking about the hotcakes. Hotcakes were her very favorite. She loved to drop a pat of butter on the steaming cakes and watch it melt and slide from the top round cake right down to the bottom. Then she'd pour sugar syrup over the top of the stack and eat them before the syrup ever had a chance to drizzle off the hotcakes onto her plate. Her stomach rumbled just imagining it.

Caroline quickly pulled her apron over her head and turned to help Eliza while Martha dressed. As soon as Martha finished tying her apron strings, the three girls rushed down the stairs to the kitchen, Caroline leading the way.

The fire in the hearth hissed and popped, and the kitchen glowed as firelight mixed with the early-morning sunshine that now poured through the windowpanes. Grandma rocked slowly in front of the fire, singing softly to baby Thomas and bouncing him on her knees.

"Good morning, Grandma," Caroline and Martha sang out.

"Good morning, dears." Grandma smiled. The rocking chair groaned and continued rocking as she stood up, opened the front of the settle, and set Thomas down inside it to play. Pulling a hairbrush from her apron pocket, she beckoned to the girls. "Come. Let's braid your hair so you'll be all ready for breakfast."

One by one, Caroline, Eliza, and Martha sat on Grandma's lap as she brushed and braided their hair. Martha and Eliza had two braids each. Only Caroline had one long braid.

Joseph was busy stirring the logs beneath the fire, sending bursts of sparks up the chimney with every poke. Caroline held her breath as he took hold of the iron tongs, lifted the kettle of water from the fire, and walked slowly toward the washstand. Carefully, Joseph tipped the kettle over the washbasin. Caroline was always afraid that the kettle would drop, and its steaming water would splash all over the floor. It was so heavy! Once, when the kettle was empty and cold and sitting on the floor far away from the fire, Joseph had allowed Caroline to try and lift it. No matter how hard she lifted and pulled, the kettle wouldn't budge. Caroline was glad that Joseph was there to lift the heavy things that Father used to lift. He was almost twelve years old, and far too big and strong to drop anything.

As soon as Joseph finished filling the wash-basin, Caroline dipped her hand into the soft soap that Mother had made and used the warm kettle water to wash her face and hands. She was just scooping a handful of water to rinse her face when the kitchen door flew open and banged against the wall. Henry burst into the room, carrying a load of cordwood that reached from his waist all the way up to his dimpled cheeks.

"I'm hungry!" Henry shouted as he dropped the logs in front of the wood box with a clatter.

"We have a lot more wood to fetch before we eat, Henry," Joseph warned. He was almost two years older than Henry and was always telling him what to do.

"It can wait until after breakfast," Mother decided. "Wash up, boys."

Caroline dried her face and hands and began to help Martha set the table. The tin plates and mugs were stored on the dish dresser that stood across from the hearth. Caroline could barely reach the dishes, even when she stood on the very tips of her toes. Martha could reach them, though. She handed the dishes to Caroline one by one, and Caroline hurried back and forth, placing them around the table.

The chairs were next. Because they never were all around the table unless it was meal-time, Caroline had to go to all corners of the kitchen to fetch them. Crisscrossing the room, she collected chairs that were in front of the fire, against the wall, and beside the sewing table. Caroline peered through the ladder backs, watching the flurry of activity in the kitchen, as she pushed each hickory-bark seat across the floor and set it under the table.

While Mother carried the platter of hotcakes and crisp fat pork slices from the stove to the table, Grandma filled each cup with milk.

Martha set a big bowl of applesauce and a crock of butter in the center of the table. Caroline waited impatiently, trying hard not to look at the tall, steaming stack of hotcakes.

"Bring the sugar syrup, please, Caroline," Mother said, smiling down at her. At once Caroline ran to the shelves where Mother stored her dry goods. When Mother asked her to get the sugar syrup, it meant she could pour it on her hotcakes first, before Eliza and Martha and Henry, even before Joseph! Mother knew just how much Caroline loved sugar syrup. She kept it on a shelf that Caroline could reach without even having to stand on her tiptoes.

Climbing onto her chair, Caroline set the sugar syrup right next to her plate. Each head was bowed as Mother prayed, "For this meal we are ever thankful, Lord. Amen."

Hotcakes and applesauce, butter and sugar syrup were passed from waiting hand to waiting hand. "Henry-O, give some of that to Eliza," Mother warned as Henry dropped a large dollop of sweet butter on his hotcakes. Since he and Father shared the same name, Mother always called Henry "Henry-O." To Caroline, Henry was just plain Henry.

Caroline looked at Henry's plate and hoped that she wouldn't have to share any of her butter with Eliza. It was too delicious. Grudgingly, Henry spread a tiny pat of his butter on Eliza's hotcake and observed, "I didn't take nearly as much as Father used to, Mother."

Mother's eyes were suddenly sad as she looked across the table at Henry. "I certainly hope that you don't *ever* eat as much butter as your father did, Henry-O," she replied. "Why, we'd never be able to keep any fresh butter in the house!"

"Mother, please tell the story about the day Grandma caught Father eating her biscuits!" Martha pleaded.

"I think you should ask Grandma to tell you that story, Martha," Mother answered. "After all, she was there when it happened."

"Oh yes, please, Grandma, tell us!" Caroline begged.

"Are you certain, Charlotte?" Grandma asked.

"Of course."

Grandma began speaking in her soft voice, and Caroline stopped eating so she could pay proper attention. Stories about Father were the only thing she liked better than hotcakes.

"When your father was a boy, not much bigger than you, why, he loved hot biscuits more than anything. Whenever I'd bake fresh biscuits, I'd set them out on the table to cool. At suppertime, we'd pass the biscuits around, and even though I knew I had baked a dozen, there were always only eleven biscuits in the basket. And when we'd pass the fresh butter, a good chunk was always missing from the beautiful butter print I had worked so hard to make! Every time I baked, both biscuits and butter were missing. And no one ever knew where they had gone.

"One day, I decided to catch the biscuit thief. I stood behind the door in the kitchen and watched as your father crawled across the floor in his knickers. He went right under the table, reached up, and felt around for the basket of biscuits. When he found it, he grabbed a biscuit. Then he reached up for the butter, broke a piece off, rubbed the butter on the biscuit, and popped it in his mouth."

"What did you do, Grandma?" Martha asked, her fork in midair.

"I marched right over to the table and stood in front of him. You can be sure that he crawled out from under the table right quick. I said, 'Young Henry, why have you been taking these biscuits?' "

"What did Father say?" Caroline asked eagerly.

"He said, 'I can't eat the butter all by itself, Mama, can I?' "

Henry laughed out loud. "Did he get in trouble, Grandma?"

"Well, young Henry," Grandma said, "he didn't eat any biscuits or butter for a whole month."

"A whole month?" Henry asked. Grandma nodded. Without another word, Henry spread some more of his butter on Eliza's hotcakes.

"Thank you, Henry-O," Mother said.

"A whole month without any butter!"

Caroline thought. She picked up her fork and took a big bite of her hotcakes. The butter had melted into them and now tasted almost as good as the sugar syrup.

Breakfast ended soon after Grandma Quiner's story, as there were plenty of chores to do. Joseph and Henry went off to gather more wood for the fire. Mother and Martha washed the breakfast dishes. Caroline was only five years old, and too little to wash. But she helped dry every drop of water off each plate and cup. Then she handed the dry dishes to Martha, and Martha put them back on the dish dresser.

"Time to make the beds and tidy your room, girls!" Mother said as she handed Caroline the broom and headed for the sewing table.

"I wish *I* could help bring in the wood instead of making beds," Martha whispered as she and Caroline climbed the stairs to their room. Caroline was glad that she didn't have to bring in wood for the fire, but she didn't tell Martha. Joseph and Henry always had little bits of wood and chunks of bark stuck to their shirts and trousers, and Caroline didn't want her dress to get all dirty and stuck with the splintery wood, too.

Resting the broom against the chimney, Caroline evened out the bumps in the mattress where pockets of straw had bunched up during the night. Once the mattress was flat again, she smoothed the sheet over it until all the wrinkles disappeared. Martha flung their quilt up in the air and let it float back down onto the bed. Picking loose feathers off their pillows, Caroline and Martha shook them until they were fluffy again and set them neatly at the head of the bed.

While Martha straightened nightclothes and made certain that the room was all picked up, Caroline swept the floor, the tall broomstick handle swinging back and forth above her head.

"Hurry, Caroline," Martha said as she shut the bottom dresser drawer. "I'm all finished, and I can't wait to get outside!"

Caroline was also in a hurry to get outside. The chickens were waiting to be fed. "I'm finished, too," she said to Martha. With one last look around, Martha and Caroline hurried down to the kitchen, set the broom back in its corner, and ran out the door.

Hog and Hens

The sun was beginning its climb to the top of a cloudless blue sky as Caroline followed Martha into the yard to do their outside chores. The morning chorus of robins' songs that greeted them was interrupted by the loud splitting of logs. Martha went off to the barn, and Caroline covered her ears and ducked as she ran past the woodpile, where Henry and Joseph were busy chopping wood. Wood chunks showered all around her brothers as they raised their axes high above their heads and brought them crashing down with a loud *crack!* into the centers of the logs.

17

Caroline slowed down as she neared the garden that covered nearly half of their acre of land. Rows of corn towered in front of her, their green leaves flopping like rabbits' ears. Lifting the bottom of her dress, Caroline stepped over the short stick fence that surrounded the garden. It had taken days for her and Martha to hunt for all the twisted sticks that Father and Joseph and Henry had used to build the fence. They needed to make it extra strong so it would keep any animals out. Father used to say it was hog-tight. Caroline didn't want to hunt for any more sticks for the fence, so she was very careful not to step on it or brush against it with her dress.

Pushing her way through the first row of corn, Caroline searched until she found a thick ear. Gently she pulled back its green wrapping and golden-brown strands, just far enough so that she could examine the first few square kernels of corn.

"How's it look, little Brownbraid?"

Caroline turned and looked for the voice at the end of the row. Henry's smiling face peered at her between the tall stalks. "Is it ready yet?"

Every morning before she fed the chickens, Caroline checked a few pieces of the late-summer ears to see if they were ripe, and every morning Henry waited at the end of a row to find out if the corn was ready, because he just couldn't wait to eat it. Caroline couldn't wait for the kernels to be plump and yellow, either. Corn was her favorite vegetable, and they hadn't had any for dinner or supper since they had picked and eaten their first crop three weeks ago.

"I think it's still a little bit too small," Caroline called out to Henry.

"Maybe by the end of the week!" Henry shouted hopefully. His sandy curls disappeared, and the stalks he was holding snapped back together, their yellow tassles and green leaves flapping back and forth. After smoothing the leaves back up over the kernels she had unwrapped, Caroline found another thick piece of corn, pulled the leaves down slightly, and pushed them back up again. It, too, was not quite ripe. "Oh, hurry!" Caroline thought.

Leaving the towering cornstalks behind her, Caroline carefully picked her way through the rest of the garden. She stopped in front of the rows of potatoes, onions, beets and turnips, carrots and sweet potatoes that Mother and Joseph had planted early in the spring. Caroline knew that each green bushy cap was hiding a purple, white, brown, or orange vegetable that grew in the ground, underneath the earth that covered it. Father once told her that these plants didn't like the sunshine, but Caroline didn't understand how anything wouldn't like sunshine. "Sunshine is a gift from God," Mother always said. Caroline thought so, too.

The sun was getting a little less warm now that summer was coming to an end, and Mother said they would soon begin harvesting. This year, Caroline was finally old enough to help her brothers and Martha pull the vegetables from the ground. How she wished harvest time would come, because she couldn't wait to dig into the earth and find all those pretty colored vegetables.

Caroline climbed back over the stick fence

and headed for the barn. The yard was covered with thick clusters of tall grass and wildflowers. The petals of the cowslips bent backward, their yellow pointed tips shooting out of their stems straight up to the sky. The goldenseal's broad green leaves and greenish-white flowers curtsied in the late-summer breeze. Bunches of tiny white flowers hid the twisted legs of the snakeroot that nestled close to the ground. Caroline was careful not to step on any of the flowers as she hurried to the barn.

The barn stood behind the frame house, past the woodpile and the garden. Until Caroline was three years old, the barn had been a log cabin. It was the first house she had ever lived in. The whole family had lived there—everyone except for baby Thomas, who hadn't yet been born. When Caroline was almost four years old, Father and some of the neighbors built a frame house close to the road. Just before the first snow, the Quiners left the little log cabin and moved into the roomy frame house. A few days later, Caroline watched as the front door of the log cabin crashed to the ground. Father split it into fire-wood. Then he used his axe to chop out a much larger space in the front wall of the log cabin. Once Father had fitted that open space with a new, wide door, the Quiners' old house became the barn. Even though only tools and grain and hay were stored there now, Caroline still felt a little bit like the barn was her home.

Running up to the barn door, Caroline pulled on the handle as hard as she could. The thick, heavy door scarcely budged.

"Need some help?" Joseph asked from behind her.

Caroline turned and looked up at him, shielding her eyes from the sun.

"Yes, please," she said, stepping away from the door.

Sunlight rushed into the center room as Joseph pulled the barn door open. Inside, Caroline took a deep breath and filled her lungs with the sweet smell of the fresh hay that was tossed all over the loft above her head. When the barn had been their log cabin, she and Martha, Joseph, and Henry slept in the loft. Now it was just a place for storing hay and straw.

Caroline followed Joseph into the back room, where Mother had once cooked their meals. Joseph reached for the broom that was against the far wall, leaning beside a shovel and a saw. A few baskets and two large buckets were also stored there, and Caroline picked up one of each and headed back to the center room.

"Time for me to sweep up all those splinters and wood chips we're making in the wood-pile," Joseph said. "Time for you to feed the chickens?"

Caroline nodded, her eyes shining. Tending to the chickens was her special chore.

"How many eggs do you think you'll find today?"

"Most days I find three or four," she replied. "Today, I think it'll be four."

Carrying the bucket and basket back to the center room, Caroline placed them on the ground next to the grain bin that was set beside one wall. Joseph and Henry kept the big wooden box filled with grain to feed the animals. The grain bin was only a little bit shorter than Caroline. When she stood right next to it, the heavy lid that kept it tightly closed rested just beneath her chin. Caroline knew she should ask Joseph to help her lift the lid, but he had already left the barn. Besides, she wanted to try to open it herself. With both hands, she lifted the top of the bin high above her head and tried to push it against the wall behind it, but it was just too heavy. Caroline gave up and dropped the lid. It slammed shut with a bang.

"Wait just a minute, silly!" Henry shouted as he ran into the barn. Reaching above Caroline, he flung the top of the bin up so hard that it flew up in a flash and crashed against the wall.

"A little one like you can't swing that top so high, Caroline," Henry said.

"It's just a little bit heavy, Henry," Caroline answered. "I almost did it."

"It has to be heavy, or it can't keep all the mice in this barn from eating supper in it!" Henry grinned.

Caroline wondered why mice would take all

the trouble to climb into a grain bin if they could just eat some of the grain that she scattered in the yard every morning, but she didn't ask Henry. She simply decided that this morning she'd leave a little extra grain for the hungry mice.

"I'm looking for Hog, Caroline. Have you seen him?" Henry asked, checking all around. Hog was the Quiners' big pig, and it was Henry's job to take care of him.

"No, Henry," Caroline answered. "I didn't see him in the yard or near the garden."

"I hope he's not off in the woods somewhere!" Henry rolled his eyes. "He'll just have to wait for his breakfast 'til I finish splitting the firewood. Holler if you see him, little Brownbraid."

As Henry ran off, Caroline began filling the bucket with grain from the bin. Even though the iron ladle scooped up more grain, she always used her hands to fill the bucket. The soft bits of corn and bran tickled her palms as they slid into the bucket, and left her fingers dusty and fresh smelling.

After she filled half of the bucket, Caroline pulled the lid of the grain bin away from the wall and stepped back as it fell down into place with a thud. Picking up the bucket of grain and her empty basket, Caroline headed back into the sunshine and around the corner, where the tiny henhouse nestled up against the barn.

A wooden peg on the door kept the henhouse snugly closed. Caroline twisted the peg and let the door drop gently to the ground, making a slope for the hens. "Morning, hens!" she called. "Sorry it took me so long, but I had to check the corn before I came to feed you. It's still not ripe."

The hens poked their brown- and gold-feathered heads out of their house and immediately began squawking at Caroline as they hopped and fluttered down the open door and onto the ground. Scooping a handful of grain from the bucket, she scattered it in a circle in front of the henhouse.

"Here's your breakfast, hens," she called. "I had hotcakes and sugar syrup this morning."

The hens waddled and squawked, their red

crowns bobbing up and down as they picked at the kernels of grain and scratched in the dirt for bugs and seeds.

"You're not talking to those silly hens again, are you?"

Martha was standing behind Caroline, holding a bucket filled with acorns and beechnuts. A few strands of her long brown hair had escaped from her braids and were blowing around her face.

"You don't think they'll talk back, do you?" she teased.

"Course not! I just wonder what they're saying to each other, that's all."

"Oh, Caroline!" Martha laughed. "Mother's waiting for the eggs, and I have to get Henry more acorns and beechnuts to feed Hog. Hurry and bring the eggs in the house, so you can help me. I'll keep hunting 'til you're ready."

"I'll hurry," Caroline said.

Martha disappeared into the barn and was back in a flash, an empty bucket swinging from her hand, as she ran toward the road in front of the frame house.

"If Henry asks, I left the first bucket of acorns by the grain bin," Martha called, hens scattering and shrieking as she passed them. "Meet me in the woods at the end of the road when you're done."

Caroline was eager to run off to the woods with Martha and search for acorns and beech-nuts to feed Hog. But first she needed to finish with the chickens. Reaching back into the bucket, she tossed a few more handfuls of grain on the ground. As soon as a small circle of earth was well sprinkled with grain and the hens were eating more than complaining, Caroline clapped her dusty hands together and picked up the empty basket she'd left on the ground. She peered through the open door of the henhouse at the slatted nesting boxes that sat on the shelf. Ever so carefully, she reached inside and ran her fingers through the straw in each box. The straw scratched and tickled her fingers as she searched for eggs. One, two, three. Four. Five! Five eggs! Caroline almost shouted with delight. Five eggs! Mother would be so happy!

Leaving the eggs safely in their boxes for a moment, Caroline tugged some tall grass from the ground and made a small green nest in her basket. Then she took each egg out of its nesting box and cushioned it in the soft grass. She was turning to bring her basket back to Mother when a loud *bang, bang, bang!* inside the barn made her jump and nearly drop all her precious eggs.

Heart pounding, Caroline set the basket beside the henhouse, ran around the corner and through the open doors of the barn. There, next to the grain bin, she saw Hog's round gray bottom and back legs. His long snout was stuck firmly in the bucket of nuts that Martha had placed beside the grain bin, and he was flinging his head back and forth furiously, slamming the bucket against the bin as he tossed and turned. Acorns and beechnuts rattled inside the bucket as Hog tried desperately to shake the bucket off his snout.

"Oh, poor Hog!" Caroline cried. She ran out of the barn, past the hens, through the wildflowers, past the garden, and stopped, all out of breath, in front of the woodpile.

"Henry! Joseph! Come quick!" Caroline screamed.

Henry and Joseph dropped their axes and ran toward Caroline.

"It's Hog," Caroline said, trying to catch her breath. "In the barn . . ."

Joseph and Henry ran ahead of Caroline, straight to the barn. By the time she caught up with them, Joseph was holding on to Hog's bottom and belly as Henry stood in front of him trying to grab the swinging bucket. Finally Henry knelt down, hugged the squirming, squealing Hog closely around the neck with one arm, and yanked the wooden bucket off his head with the other. Acorns and beechnuts flew every which way, and Caroline ducked until they had all fallen to the ground.

"Easy, Hog," Henry said, patting Hog's side and rubbing his smooth gray back. Hog lifted his head and stretched his neck. Then he bent down and with a snuffle and snort started eating the acorns and beechnuts that lay at his feet.

"How did these nuts get into the barn?" Joseph asked.

"Martha left them in a bucket by the grain bin so Henry could feed Hog," Caroline answered reluctantly, trying not to giggle. Now that the excitement was over, she couldn't help but remember how funny Hog looked with a bucket stuck on his nose.

"Next time she ought to leave the bucket on top of the bin," Joseph said sternly, and left the barn.

Henry looked over at Caroline, his eyes merry. "I guess Hog never wandered off to the woods, after all," he said. "Thanks for finding him, little Brownbraid."

Kneeling down, Henry began filling the empty bucket with the acorns that were scattered all over the ground, and Caroline hurried to help him gather the stray nuts that had flown into every corner.

"Sorry, Hog. You can't eat all of these at once," Henry said as he led Hog into the yard.

Caroline followed Henry and Hog into the sunlight. She wished Henry would let Hog eat whatever he wanted. Maybe then he wouldn't think about how much his head was hurting.

Five feathered hens clucked, flapped their wings, and strutted on the dirt as Caroline walked back to the henhouse and reached for her basket of eggs. The sun had kept the eggs and their grass nest warm while she had been away. Five eggs! Caroline smiled proudly and hurried back toward the house, holding her basket of eggs tightly. Five whole eggs! She must tell Mother!

Wash Day

Cool water jumped and splashed from one side of the bucket to the other, sloshing over the sides and onto the dry grass. The wooden handle dug into Caroline's fingers as she lugged the heavy bucket past the barn and the henhouse. Just yesterday she was in such a hurry to show Mother the five eggs she had collected, that her bare feet practically flew through the grass and wildflowers. Today, her trek across the yard seemed to take forever. She tried to hold the bucket away from her skirt and apron, so the water wouldn't soak her clothes along with the grass.

Martha trudged along beside Caroline. She also carried a bucket, but it was much bigger than Caroline's. With every step, Martha was drenching her apron and the grass around her with water that flip-flopped out of her bucket.

"When I'm a grown lady," Martha exclaimed, "I'm going to have so many dresses, I'll never have to wash them! I'll just wear a different one every day."

Caroline looked up at her big sister. Martha's bonnet was still tied, but it had fallen off her head and hung down past her shoulders. Her forehead was damp, and her dark eyes snapped. Even her braids were swinging impatiently. Caroline and Martha had already been to the well four times, and Caroline was afraid that they had many more trips to make before Mother had enough water to do the week's washing.

Caroline tried to concentrate on having so many pretty dresses, but all she could think about was her fingers. "Do your fingers hurt, Martha?" Caroline asked.

"My fingers . . . and my hands, and my arms!"

Martha grumbled. "I hate wash day. I'd rather do *anything* than help Mother on wash day."

"Maybe this will be enough water for now," Caroline hoped aloud.

"Goodness glory, Martha!" Mother looked up as Caroline and Martha pushed through the kitchen door and gratefully set their buckets down in front of the hearth. "If you spill any more water on your apron, I won't have to bother washing it!"

"I'm sorry," Martha said, wrinkling her nose and looking up at Mother. "I cannot keep all the water from splashing out of the bucket! No matter how hard I try!"

"Carry a little less at a time, dear," Mother answered calmly. She reached for their buckets and poured the water into the big iron pot that hung from the swinging crane on the hearth.

"Are you feeling tired yet, Caroline?" Mother looked down at Caroline. Caroline had never before helped Martha carry water from the well because Mother did not think she was big and strong enough. But today Caroline had begged to help, and Mother had agreed.

"I still want to help," Caroline answered. But she *was* tired. Her arms tingled, and her fingers were stiff. Even her back hurt a little. She hadn't realized how hard carrying the water would be.

"I want to help, too!" Eliza ran across the room and tugged on Mother's skirt.

"You're not yet big enough to help me wash clothes, Eliza," Mother said. "But you are big enough to be a wonderful helper for Grandma. Please go and see if she needs help with baby Thomas."

As Eliza skipped away, Mother turned back to Caroline. "You may still help, Caroline," she said. "But I think we will have the boys haul water for a while. You and Martha may carry in wood for the fire."

Rubbing her sore hands together, Caroline looked over at Martha. She wasn't sure if carrying wood was better than carrying water.

But Martha was sure. "Come on, Caroline!" She tugged at her sister's arm and hurried her out the door. "We can bring in the wood, just like Joseph and Henry always do!"

Caroline followed Martha as she bustled to the woodpile. Joseph and Henry were busy gathering together all the wood they had just finished chopping.

"Mother says it's your turn to carry water from the well now," Martha announced. "Caroline and I will bring the wood inside."

"You're driving your duck to the wrong pond again, Miss Martha!" Henry teased. "This wood is far too heavy for you to carry."

"I'm almost as strong as you!" Martha shouted back.

"Of course you are," Joseph soothed Martha, as Henry burst into laughter. Grabbing hold of his brother's arm, he added, "Let's go. Mother's going to need that water right away."

"I'll show that Henry," Martha exclaimed as her brothers disappeared.

Holding her apron out with one hand, Martha began piling kindling and wood chips on it with the other. Caroline was glad that she no longer had to carry the heavy bucket of water. She was glad that her fingers would soon stop being so sore. But as she watched

Martha, she suddenly wasn't sure about carrying sticks and dirty wood on her apron. She had tried so hard to keep it clean. Now Mother would have to wash it, too.

Caroline and Martha made trip after trip to the woodpile and back, filling their aprons and then the wood box. Mother needed plenty of wood to keep the fire constantly leaping beneath the big iron pot. The water in the pot must continue boiling for as long as she washed clothes. Time after time during wash day, Mother checked the wood box to make certain that it was stacked with wood. Now it was Caroline and Martha's job to make certain that whenever Mother looked, the wood box was full.

Once the water in the pot was steaming and bubbling, Mother called Martha into the kitchen. "I'm ready to begin the wash, Martha," Mother told her as Joseph pushed another log onto the fire. "Please practice your Bible verses while you're waiting for your clothes."

Martha heaved a great sigh. "Already, Mother?"

Mother wiped her brow and paused a moment to look at her oldest daughter. "Your clothes will be clean and dry in no time, Martha," she said firmly. "Caroline, go upstairs with your sister and bring me her clothes. Into your flannels, please, Martha."

"Oh, why is it always sunny on the day Mother does the wash?" Martha whispered dejectedly as she and Caroline climbed the stairs. "I want to be outside today! I don't want to sit in bed and practice silly verses!"

"The sunshine will help dry your dress fast," Caroline said cheerfully, trying to make Martha feel better. Every week on wash day, Caroline felt extra sorry for Martha because she had to climb into bed and stay there until her dress and apron were cleaned. Martha only had one everyday dress to wear, and Mother wouldn't allow her to wear her Sunday dress for anything but church. Usually Caroline didn't like to wear Martha's old dresses, but on wash day, she was glad that she had two everyday dresses to wear, even if they were hand-me-downs. At least she didn't have to stay in bed while Mother washed.

Caroline picked up all the dirty clothes in their room, added Martha's clothes to the pile in her arms, and clattered down the stairs. As she peered around her heap of dirty laundry, she found Mother kneeling beside the washtub in front of the fire. Mother was reaching into an old pan with an iron ladle and emptying several ladlefuls of thick, runny soap into the washtub.

"Thank you, Caroline." Mother smiled as she looked up from her work. "You may set those by the other pile of clothes."

As Caroline dropped the clothes on the floor, she smelled a sharp odor that reminded her of spoiled apple jelly. Crinkling her nose, Caroline asked, "Mother, why does soap smell so bad?"

"Because I added borax and ammonia to the soap to make certain that our clothes come clean," Mother said. "It's terrible, isn't it?"

"Awful!" agreed Henry, who had just dropped another bucket of water in front of the hearth.

Mother looked up from the washtub and checked the wood box. "Henry," she said, "we'll soon need more wood for the fire. And when you and Joseph are done with that, we need more water to boil and rinse the clothes."

"Yes, ma'am," Henry said, and ran out the door.

"Caroline, make two piles of clothes for me, please," Mother said. "The first one should have all the white clothes, the other all the colored clothes."

Caroline sat down in the middle of the floor, surrounded by a big pile of dresses and trousers, skirts and blouses, socks and long underwear. She carefully sorted each piece into one of the two piles.

"That's fine," Mother said. "Now hand me the white clothes, one at a time."

Caroline passed Martha's apron to Mother and watched as she plunged it into the washtub, which was now full of bubbles, pulled it out of the water, dripping and covered with suds, and spread it on the ribbed washstick. Mother then scrubbed the apron as hard as she could, plunged it into the soapy water, spread it on the washstick, and scrubbed it again. When Mother finished scrubbing all the white clothes, she carried them to the hearth and dropped them into the boiling water, one by one. Standing over the iron pot, she stirred the boiling water with a long stick. It seemed to Caroline that Mother stirred those clothes forever. Finally, she lifted them out of the hot, soapy water with the long stirring stick and carefully dropped them into an empty tub waiting close to the hearth.

Reaching into the tub and gently squeezing the soapy water out of the white clothes, Mother looked up at Caroline. "I'm almost ready for the colored clothes," she said. "Please pile them next to the washtub."

Caroline carried all the dark trousers, the blue and brown and red print dresses, and the flannel socks and shirts to the tub of soapy water and began handing them to Mother. The soap squeaked and squished as Mother scrubbed the wet clothes against the ribbed wood of the washstick. Once they were scrubbed clean and Mother had stirred them for a long time, she turned to Caroline and said, "Please run and call the boys, Caroline. It's time to empty this tub."

Caroline ran out to the woodpile. The warm breeze cooled her face, and she wiped away little drops of moisture that had gathered on her forehead from the steam rising out of the iron pot. Henry and Joseph were pulling together more split logs for the fire, and Caroline waved to them to stop.

"Mother said to come empty the water!" she shouted.

Joseph nodded and bent down to pick up one last log. "Come help us, Caroline. You can carry the small pieces of wood."

Caroline held out her arms while Joseph placed a few thin logs on top of them. They all walked slowly toward the house, trying not to drop any of the firewood.

"Sometimes I wish Martha wasn't the only one with one change of clothes," Henry said.

"Why?" Caroline asked, surprised.

"Because then I could stay in bed instead of

working! Better than that, I'd just roam the woods in my flannels 'til all my clothes were dry! As awful hot and itchy as they may be, it would still be better than working or lying around in bed." Henry looked at Caroline, a mischievous warning in his eyes. "Don't tell Mother, Caroline."

"I don't think Martha likes staying in bed, Henry," Caroline said. "And neither would I," she added firmly, pushing past him into the house. She dropped her load of wood into the wood box.

"Good. You're here, Joseph," Mother said. Together they carefully lifted the steaming iron pot off the swinging crane and away from the hearth.

"Open the door, Caroline. Hurry!" Mother said.

Caroline ran and held the kitchen door open as Mother and Joseph carried the heavy pot outside. Setting it down on a thick patch of grass, they tipped it over. Soapy water gushed out of the pot onto the grass and dirt and swelled into a mighty puddle of bubbles and foam.

"Let's get this back in the house," Mother said. She took a rag and wiped the inside of the iron pot clean. Caroline held the kitchen door open once again while Mother and Joseph carried the pot back to the hearth, pulled out the swinging crane, and set the pot safely on its hook.

"We'll need more water now," Mother said. "Can you help Henry and me carry some, Caroline, so Joseph can keep up with the wood?"

Rubbing her sore hands together, Caroline answered, "Yes, Mother."

Mother, Caroline, and Henry returned to the well and began carrying bucket after bucket of water back into the house. Caroline's hands were red and burning when the iron pot was finally full again.

Mother poured the last bucket of water into the iron pot and moved the swinging crane slowly back over the fire. Wiping her hand across her brow, she said brightly, "Let's eat now and give this water a chance to boil! Grandma surely has dinner ready."

Grandma had prepared plenty of baked beans and pork, sweet potatoes, cheese, and corn bread. For the first time that morning, the harsh odor of soap didn't sting Caroline's nose as she breathed. The fresh, warm smells of Grandma's cooking filled the air instead.

"Thank you, Mother Quiner. This all looks delicious," Mother said as she finished putting food on a plate for Martha. "Caroline, I'll help Grandma set the table while you take this upstairs."

Step after careful step, Caroline climbed the stairs, balancing Martha's plate of food in one hand and holding her cup of milk tightly in the other. The cool tin cup soothed her stinging palm and fingers.

When Martha heard footsteps on the stairs, she hurriedly began reciting her Bible verses.

"Here's dinner, Martha." Caroline handed her the plate and cup and waited by the edge of the bed.

Martha sat up in her red flannels. "Oh, I hate wearing this," she said, scratching the back of her neck. "It itches, and it's so hot! I wish I could wear nothing at all while my clothes get washed." Flopping back on the pillows, Martha looked intently at her little sister. "Is Mother almost finished washing my dress?" she asked.

"Almost. Once the water boils again, she'll start rinsing all the clothes."

"Rinse?" Martha cried out. "You mean the clothes aren't even rinsed yet, Caroline?"

"No." Caroline shook her head. "Mother's about to rinse them now. Then we have to put them outside to dry. The sun is so hot today, Martha, your dress will dry in no time!"

Martha crossed her arms. "When Father was still here, I always had more than one dress to wear."

"I wish he was here, too," Caroline whispered.

"Caroline!"

Caroline jumped when she heard Mother calling from the room below. "I'll bring your dress as soon as it's dry!" she promised Martha as she ran down the stairs.

"You're slower than an earthworm, little Brownbraid!" Henry called from his seat at the table. "Hurry! I'm starving!"

Sitting down, Caroline waited as Mother and Grandma filled her plate with the hot, delicious food. After just one bite, she forgot her aching hands and hungry stomach.

So did Henry. He was just about to pop a whole piece of corn bread in his mouth when Mother looked his way. "Henry-O Quiner!" she admonished. "Break that corn bread into pieces before you eat it."

"Yes, ma'am." Dimples flashing, Henry did as he was told.

Mother had just turned her attention back to baby Thomas when Henry blurted out, "Please, Grandma, may I have some more beans and pork?"

Mother looked sternly at Henry. "How many times must I tell you, Henry-O, that you are never to ask for more food at this table? You must wait until the food is offered to you."

"Yes, ma'am," Henry said. Grandma waited a moment before she served second helpings, and before long everyone was feeling full and refreshed.

As soon as Caroline finished drying the last cup and plate from dinner, Mother called her back to the hearth. "The water is beginning to boil, Caroline," she said. "We're ready to rinse the clothes."

Mother began by dropping the big pile of wet white clothing into the pot of clear, boiling water. First she stirred the white clothes with the long stick until they were rinsed clean. Once they were cleansed of any dirt or soap, Mother pulled each piece from the boiling rinse with the stick, dropped it into an empty tub, and then wrung it tightly until every drop she could squeeze out had dripped into the tub.

Long strands of Mother's black hair had escaped from her bun and were pasted against her forehead and neck by the time she finished rinsing all the clothes. She pushed the strands to the side of her face as she, Caroline, Henry, and Joseph began carrying big baskets full of wet clothing out into the yard.

"Goodness glory, these baskets are heavy today," Mother said as they dropped them on the grass. Pulling the clean clothes out of the basket, Mother and Joseph shook each piece a final time. Caroline closed her eyes tight as the clothes snapped loudly and a spray of water droplets flew into the air.

As Mother and Joseph finished shaking the clothes, they handed them one by one to Caroline and Henry. It was their job to find a soft grassy spot to lay each piece neatly to dry.

Tall blades of grass swayed slowly back and forth around the wet clothes. Beneath her bonnet, Caroline felt the heavy heat of the sun. She hoped the hot sunshine and the gentle breeze would dry all the clothes soon so that she could bring Martha her clean, dry dress.

"I suppose we'll have to let the sun finish the job now, won't we, Caroline?" Mother asked as she stood rubbing her hands together. Henry and Joseph had just collected the empty baskets and carried them back to the house. Looking around at all the clean clothes drying on the soft grass, Mother smiled wearily and lifted Caroline's chin. "You've been such a big help today, Caroline. I think we just may have to use some of those fine eggs you gathered yesterday to make a special treat for after supper."

Caroline smiled and tucked her hand securely in Mother's. As they walked back to the frame house, Mother gently squeezed her sore fingers. Their walk across the yard didn't take very long at all.

Stagecoach

Grandma looked up from her needle-point. "You're leaving for town now, Charlotte?" she asked.

"Yes, Mother Quiner," Mother answered. She picked up an empty jug and basket lying next to the dish dresser and set them on a chair beside the sewing table. "I've called Martha in to help with Eliza and Thomas."

Caroline sat next to Grandma, busily working on her sampler. Summer had eased into fall, and Caroline had begun to spend many more afternoons sitting at the sewing table and practicing her stitches with Grandma. She had been sewing ever since she was four years old, and she had already learned from Mother and Grandma how to sew many different kinds of stitches. Pushing and pulling a long strand of thread in and out of the heavy linen, she was careful not to poke her fingers with the sharp needle that held the thread. Still sometimes she wished she had a thimble to wear on all her fingers instead of just one.

As she tucked her hair neatly into her bonnet, Mother looked over Caroline's bent head. "You've nearly finished *F*, Caroline!" she said in surprise. "And your stitches are lovely!"

Caroline felt her cheeks flush as she smiled down at her sampler. She had learned three new stitches since Mother had last viewed her progress. "Thank you, Mother," she said. "Grandma just taught me this new stitch."

"I think it won't be long now, Mother Quiner, until we are ready to frame Caroline's sampler," Mother said. Patting Caroline's shoulder, she added, "You're stitching so fast, you'll finish your alphabet in no time."

Caroline had only finished *A*, *B*, *C*, *D* and *E*, each in a different stitch. She knew that she had many more stitches to learn and practice before she finished every letter of the alphabet on her sampler. But Mother's praise made her even more eager to sew all those letters. "Mother likes my stitches!" she thought, glowing with pride. Mother, who made the prettiest and most perfect stitches of all.

"If you hurry and finish that *F*, Caroline," Mother said, "you may come along to town."

Caroline looked up excitedly. "I'll hurry," she said.

"I'll go find Henry, then. We'll wait for you in front of the house."

Mother closed the door tightly behind her, and Caroline pulled her thread back and forth through the stiff cloth of her sampler as fast as her fingers would go. Grandma quietly worked on her own needlework, watching from the corner of her eye as Caroline quickly finished her last two stitches.

"That looks just fine, Caroline," Grandma said. "Go now. I'll put your sampler away."

Folding the cloth in half with the stitched letters on the inside, Caroline handed it to Grandma with her needle and thread. "Thank you, Grandma," she said, and ran up to her room to get her white bonnet from the chest.

Caroline hadn't been to town since the springtime. Even though it was not quite two miles from the Quiners' frame house, Mother visited town far less often than Father used to. "Too busy and crowded!" Mother would say whenever she returned from a trip to town. Father had always loved the hustle and bustle. When he was trading, picking up supplies, or inspecting a new house or shop he had helped build, he often took Caroline along with him. "This town's grown up same as you, Caroline," he'd tell her as they arrived at the crossroads of the two main roads in Brookfield. Shaking his head, Father would marvel at the small cluster of houses and shops. "Day you were born wasn't but a hundred folks or so this part of Wisconsin," he'd say. "My guess is there's ten times that now for certain. Just look at it! A regular little town!" Caroline would then feel Father's gentle tug on her braid. "With any luck, you won't grow up quite so fast, my little Brownbraid."

Caroline hurried down the stairs, tying her bonnet strings tightly beneath her chin. She couldn't wait to get to the busy town and see all the buildings and people. And it was always a special treat to explore the grocer's shelves.

She kissed Grandma on the cheek and rushed outside to find Mother. Though the sunshine was warm, there was a crisp autumn breeze that tossed her bonnet strings and chilled her cheeks. Caroline shivered and was glad that she was wearing her blue wool dress with long sleeves.

Henry emerged from the back of the house, wiping his brow and straightening his red flannel shirt as he followed Mother's quick steps.

"You look very nice, Caroline," Mother said, examining her closely before she turned to Henry. "Now, Henry-O," she said, brushing stray chips of wood off his shirt, "if you could only straighten those curls some."

"Like this?" Henry asked. He pulled the

tips of his sandy curls down toward his chin until the crinkly lines of hair became straight. Caroline had never seen Henry look so silly, and she tried very hard not to giggle.

"That's quite enough, Henry Odin Quiner." Mother shook her head and sighed, but her eyes were smiling. "Hurry and get the ashes over there." Mother pointed to the gray burlap sack resting beside the front door of the house. "I hope it isn't too heavy for you to carry, Henry-O. We'll walk along slowly while you drag it, and we shouldn't be in any danger of breaking it open."

Henry's curls bounced back in place as he winked at Caroline and ran to get the sack. Twisting the corner of the sack into a handle that he could hold securely, he pulled the ashes carefully across the grass and down to the street.

They walked slowly down the dirt road, past several houses made of logs, frame, and slab. Like the Quiners, many of their neighbors had built frame houses close to the road and now used their old log cabins as barns and stables.

All along the roadside, bunches of white, purple, blue, and lavender asters rocked in the wind. Towering regally above the houses, enormous oaks reminded all who passed of the magnificent forests that had once claimed the land where rows of houses and cabins now stood. The cool wind sailed through their branches, setting their leaves free to float lazily to the ground like golden snowflakes.

Dry red, yellow, and brown leaves danced all along the road. Caroline felt them crunching beneath her feet and remembered how much Father had loved walking on the fallen autumn leaves and listening to them crackle. Just last fall, Caroline had watched delightedly as he pulled off his boots and jumped into a pile of leaves, crunching them into crisp, dusty bits with his bare toes. Caroline took a deep breath of the crisp fall air and wondered if the leaves reminded Mother of Father, too. The last time the leaves had all dropped, Father had left on his voyage. Caroline struggled to keep tears from slipping down her cheeks and tried to think about how exciting it was to be heading toward town. If Mother wasn't remembering Father right now, Caroline didn't want to remember and be sad, either.

"Johnny O'Leary, move that log away, now!" A loud, angry voice made Caroline jump and forget her sadness at once. They had just arrived at the crossroads of the town, and it was screaming and jumping and hurrying all around them. A large group of men and boys, busy building a new structure on one corner, worked and half listened as a burly man with a stubbly beard barked orders at them. Some of the men were chopping and splitting wood; others were hauling stone. The noise was deafening, and Caroline clapped her hands over her ears. Never before had the town seemed so loud and busy. Caroline moved closer to Mother's skirt and hurried along behind her, her shoes now kicking up dust instead of crunching leaves.

"Goodness glory!" Mother raised her voice so she could be heard above the chopping axes and crashing stones. "Another tavern! What we need in this town is another schoolhouse!"

Mother started across the busy street, but then stopped so suddenly that Caroline crashed into her and almost fell backward. A thunderous roar shook the street. Henry released the bag of ashes and grabbed Caroline's arm. Pulling her away from Mother's black wool skirt, he held her so tightly she could hardly move.

"Stay where you are, Caroline," Mother warned loudly. She, too, stepped back and held her arm out in front of Caroline and Henry.

"What is it, Henry?" Caroline asked, struggling to see around Mother's arm. "What's making all that noise?"

"It's the stagecoach!" Henry shouted.

The dust from the road swirled up toward Caroline's chin in thick, choking gray clouds. Two huge black horses snorted and strained as they led a great team of horses, one white and three brown, past the Quiners. Caroline stood on her tiptoes and stared up in wonder. A sea of faces above her looked as though they were riding right through the air. Beards and hats and a bonnet or two all mixed together with the blue sky and puffy white clouds.

"Who-o-o-o-a! Who-o-o-o-a!"

Caroline jumped, and Henry's hand tightened on her shoulder as the loudest man's voice she had ever heard roared at them out of nowhere. All at once the team of horses lurched backward and stopped.

"E-e-e-asy girls, eeeeea-sy!" the voice hollered again. Then it began clucking at the horses.

Stomping and grunting, the horses whinnied and stamped ahead slowly. The faces Caroline had seen above her were now people perched on the top of the stagecoach.

"Who-o-o-a!" the man grumbled, and the horses stopped completely. Caroline found the face that belonged with the voice: a black-bearded face in a black hat.

The stagecoach now stood directly in front of Caroline. She had seen stagecoaches on her trips to town before, but she had never been so close to one. She looked up at the giant iron wheels in astonishment. The front wheel was as tall as she was, and the back wheel was even taller. Thick leather straps were slung over the axles, and between and above the wheels, the coach hovered like a huge, brown wooden box. The flat top was loaded with people and luggage. The black-bearded man with the loud voice was seated on top of the coach, right in front. Two other men sat with him, one on either side.

"Stop! Brookfield!" the black-bearded man called out.

"That's the driver," Henry whispered in Caroline's ear.

The driver jumped from the top of the coach down to the dusty street. He opened the coach door right in front of Caroline, and she stood on her tiptoes to peek inside. Two benches at the front and back were packed tight with passengers. More travelers sat on a third bench in the middle of the coach, talking excitedly.

The door opened, and passengers began pouring out. Men in suit coats and wide-brimmed hats jumped out into the street first. Some then turned back to help the women passengers, in their dark dresses and bonnets, step down from the coach.

"Baggage!" the driver bellowed as he helped the last passenger down from the roof. Climbing back up to the top of the stagecoach, he began tugging at the bags. Passengers hurried to claim their belongings and headed up and down the street.

One short woman wearing a long black coat and a fancy black hat stood beside Henry and chattered loudly to her companion as they waited for their bags. "I thought we'd *never* arrive in this dreadful place, William!" she seethed. "I couldn't have possibly survived one more bump! What terrible roads! We never, *ever* had such horrid drives in the coaches in New York!"

The short woman did not notice Caroline or Henry as she gathered up her skirts, lifted her nose high in the air, and strutted off. "She's so awful," Caroline whispered loudly to Henry as they watched the woman and her friend disappear down the road.

"Mail!" the driver now called as he struggled to pull the last heavy sack from the top of the coach.

"Look, Caroline." Mother's voice turned Caroline's attention back to the stagecoach. "This stagecoach brings all the mail to Wisconsin from Boston and New Haven."

Mail! Caroline loved to hear Mother read the mail that Grandmother and Grandfather Tucker sent from Boston almost as much as Mother loved reading it. Imagine that all those letters had to travel so far and over so many bumpy roads to get to Mother! It was no wonder letters were so precious.

"I think we've seen enough, children," Mother said. "Come along now."

Before Mother could take a step, the largest black horse on the team lunged ahead restlessly. It was just enough to throw the driver off balance, and he shouted as he fell toward the rail of the baggage rack and dropped the sack of mail. Bulging at all corners, the gray canvas sack flew through the air and landed with a loud thud and a puff of dust on the ground in front of Caroline and Henry. Envelopes and packages scattered like leaves across the dusty road. Steadying himself, the driver jumped down from the stagecoach, landing in the midst of all the fallen mail. He dropped to his knees and started tossing the dusty letters and packages back into the bag. A crowd of townsfolk gathered all around him, peering down at the letters to see if any belonged to them.

"Caroline," Mother said briskly, "we must leave now. Don't forget the sack of ashes, Henry-O."

"But, Mother," Caroline asked, "shouldn't we stay to see if there is a letter for us?"

"Not in all this commotion. If we have a letter, it'll be delivered to the grocer's as it always is. Perhaps even while we are there."

Reluctantly, Caroline followed Mother and Henry as they left the crowd and headed toward the grocer's. She couldn't help but look back over her shoulder at the stagecoach, the

fallen mail, the great team of horses, the passengers in their dark clothes. How exciting it
must be to journey to new places! Maybe she
would travel on a stagecoach someday, too.
Maybe she could even sit on the roof.

The Grocer's Shelves

Caroline held Mother's hand tightly and squinted as she walked across the dusty road. All the busy horses and wagons going about their business in town had kicked up great pockets of dirt, and swirling clouds of dust tickled her nose. Caroline rubbed her stinging eyes as they passed the wagonmaker's, a blacksmith's shop, a noisy, crowded tavern, and the shoemaker's house. Finally they arrived at the grocer's door.

"Come along, Henry-O," Mother said as she crossed the wooden plank sidewalk. Smiling and nodding, she excused herself through the crowd of chattering men and women clustered outside the general store sharing the news of the day.

Dragging the heavy sack of ashes through the crowd, Henry made sure he didn't bump into anyone. Caroline followed right behind, watching the ground and the bottom of the sack in case any of the ashes seeped out. She had no choice but to walk through the dust in the street, but she didn't have to get ashes on her shoes if she could help it. These shoes had belonged to Martha not long ago, and were worn and stained in spots. Still, they didn't pinch her toes as her last pair had, and Caroline wanted them to stay as nice as they could until her feet outgrew them.

Caroline was so busy watching the sack of ashes, she didn't notice that she was inside the general store until she suddenly found herself surrounded by a long gray skirt, a long black skirt, and two pairs of brown trousers.

"Good day, Sarah. Good day, Benjamin," Mother greeted the woman in the gray skirt and the man standing next to her.

"A fine day to you, Charlotte! How's the likes of you?" a man's voice boomed cheerfully.

Caroline looked up and saw that one of the skirts and a pair of the trousers belonged to Mr. and Mrs. Carpenter. The Carpenters lived two houses away from the Quiners, and they were Caroline's favorite neighbors. Father and Mr. Carpenter had settled in Brookfield at the same time and helped clear each other's land and build their log cabins and frame houses. In the winter, Caroline could see the roof of the Carpenters' tall frame house from her bedroom window. Mrs. Carpenter often spent the day with Mother when Mr. Carpenter and their son, Charles, went off hunting or fishing with Father, Joseph, and Henry. Martha always asked to go along on these fishing and hunting trips, but Mother always said no. Caroline felt sorry for Martha, because she knew that Martha loved to be with Joseph and Henry. But even more than that, Martha loved to be around Charlie Carpenter. Charlie was always making funny faces, telling silly jokes, and teasing Martha.

Since Father went away, Mr. Carpenter often visited and helped Henry and Joseph with heavy chores. He and Charles still took them along on fishing and hunting trips, and Mother still wouldn't let Martha go along.

Mother spoke quietly with Mrs. Carpenter as Mr. Carpenter knelt down in front of Caroline. The sleeves of his blue flannel shirt were pushed up to his elbows, and he rested his big, strong hands on his knees as he looked at Caroline. "Well, hello there!" he said. Thick layers of his long brown hair fell in front of his dark eyes, but Caroline could still see the deep lines around his dark eyes crinkle when he smiled. "How is our little Brownbraid today?"

Mr. Carpenter had called Caroline "little Brownbraid" from the moment he first heard Father say it. His kind voice and eyes always made her feel happy, but whenever he was around, she missed Father even more. Caroline especially missed the crinkles that would appear around Father's laughing eyes whenever he told a funny story or pulled her high up in his arms to hug her.

"Hello, Mr. Ben," Caroline answered. Although Mother never liked it when she, her brothers or Martha called Mr. Carpenter "Mr. Ben," he still insisted on it. "I'm fine, thank you."

Mr. Carpenter looked over at Henry and the bulging gray sack he had dropped at his side. "Sakes alive, that's a mighty full sack, son. What's inside?"

"Ashes, sir," Henry answered.

Mr. Carpenter nodded. "Hmmm," he said, rubbing his bearded chin, "You dragged that all the way from home?"

"Yes, sir." Henry nodded proudly. "And I didn't lose but a little."

"Good for you, son! Let me help you lift it to the counter."

Henry hesitated. "Thank you, Mr. Ben, but I can do it."

"You're stubborn as a rooster, young Henry." Mr. Carpenter slapped his knee and stood up. "I've nothing to do while I'm waiting for Sarah to finish her shopping, so come now, let me give you a hand." Leaning over, he lifted one side of the sack while Henry struggled to lift the other side. Together, they swung it up onto the long pine-board counter. A little cloud of ash puffed up around the sack as it landed with a thud.

"Trading some ash, there, Ben?" Mr. Porter, the grocer, looked up from his ledger. He was a tall man, so tall that the pots and kettles hanging from the ceiling nearly touched the shiny top of his bald head. Little tufts of gray hair hung over his ears and decorated the back of his head. The buttons of his clean white shirt and dark gray vest strained to hold in his round belly.

"Not today, Wills," Mr. Ben answered as he brushed a bit of ash off the front of his shirt. "Mr. Henry Quiner carried this here sack all the way from home."

"Well, then, you've come to the right place. I've sackfuls already to sell to the soap factory. Do me good to have even more," Mr. Porter said. Raising his furry eyebrows, he looked down at Henry. "Mr. Henry, why don't we weigh this sack and find out just how many tons of ashes you've lugged in here! Come, lad, the scale's in the back corner of the store."

Walking around the counter, the grocer smiled at Mother, who was still standing near the front door. "The boy and I will be weighing the ashes, Mrs. Quiner," he called. "We'll be back in no time."

"Is it all right with you if Caroline and I take a peek around the store while you two talk, Charlotte?" Mr. Carpenter asked.

"Certainly." Mother nodded. "You may go along, Caroline. Be careful not to touch anything."

"I will," Caroline said. This was one time that she was happy not to have to stand and listen to Mother's conversation. More than anything, Caroline wanted to explore the grocer's shelves.

Following Mr. Carpenter around to one side of the store, Caroline noticed that the wall in front of her looked just like one of the walls in their barn, except this wall held many, many more tools. Rakes and shovels and plows hung from it, as did hammers and knives, saws and hatchets. A big round barrel stuffed with brooms sat beside it.

"I don't believe I need any of these right now, Caroline." Mr. Carpenter gestured toward the wall. "How 'bout you?"

"Another broom would be nice, sir," Caroline answered seriously.

Taking care not to bump into any of the hanging tools, Mr. Carpenter and Caroline walked past a barrel full of nails and crates filled with sawdust. Caroline peered inside one barrel at the hundreds of shiny pointed tacks. Most of them looked brand-new, but a few had begun to turn rusty.

The cool, musty smell of the metal mixed with the smell of the sawdust in the crate beside it, and Caroline held back a sneeze. Rubbing her nose, she peered into the crate, but she could see nothing in it but sawdust.

"Why do they sell sawdust here, Mr. Ben? Does anybody buy it?" Caroline couldn't help asking.

Mr. Carpenter looked down at the crate and smiled. He dug his hand deep into the sawdust and very carefully pulled out a shiny piece of metal.

"That looks just like the ends of the axes that Henry and Joseph use to split logs!" Caroline exclaimed.

"And that's exactly what this is, Caroline. An axehead. Mr. Porter keeps a whole bunch of them in that sawdust."

As carefully as he had taken it out, Mr. Carpenter laid the axehead down and covered it with sawdust. With Caroline close on his heels, he headed toward the back of the store, where piles of empty baskets and crates, sacks and stepladders, jugs and boxes crowded the floor.

Caroline slowed down so that she could look inside the containers, but Mr. Carpenter had other plans.

"Hurry along, Caroline." Mr. Carpenter beckoned as he stepped over the boxes and crates. "Come see some of my favorite tools for the kitchen."

Standing in the very back corner of the store were tall shelves filled with wooden pails and mugs and tubs. Mr. Carpenter's eyes twinkled as he said, "Perhaps I can interest you in a piggin, a noggin, or a firkin today, miss?"

He held up a small pail from its thin wooden handle.

"I, for one, like to hide all my pieces of pie in a piggin." Then he lifted a little mug and added, "I sneak off with my piggin, and wash every bite of pie down with a nip from my noggin!" Finally, he put the pail on the floor and lifted a small tub high above his head. "And if I'm still hungry, I feast on hot bread topped with all the fresh butter my firkin can hold!"

Mr. Carpenter looked so silly holding the firkin above his head that Caroline couldn't help but giggle. "Oh, Mr. Ben! All the fresh butter in that firkin?" she asked mischievously. "You'd put all that fresh butter on one piece of bread?"

"Nothing better than fresh butter oozing down the sides of hot baked bread, I say!" Mr. Carpenter replied grandly. Returning the containers back to the shelf, he put his hand lightly on Caroline's shoulder. "Makes a man hungry just thinking about it! Now let's see what we can find in the rest of the store."

On the side of the store opposite all the hanging tools was an assortment of rifles and muskets stored in a short, wide glass case. Beside the case, a small crate filled with lead balls stood next to a large barrel that was tightly closed. Mr. Carpenter knocked on the lid of the barrel three times. "That's where the grocer keeps the gunpowder, Caroline. Right there in that keg," he said.

Caroline surveyed the keg gravely. Father used to let her and Martha watch him clean and load his gun. Joseph and Henry had often helped Father make bullets, and Caroline remembered Father's warnings to her brothers: "Never leave this rifle unloaded, sons. A rifle must always be ready to shoot." Father would load the gun and hang it from two hooks above the kitchen door of their frame house. It was now Joseph's job to make certain the gun was loaded. Mother made certain the gun was always in its place above the door.

Next to the glass gun case, another set of shelves held carefully stacked china dishes. A tall girl wearing an apron and cap and drawing water from a well was painted on a few of them, while others were painted with flowers that looked as though they were blooming right there on the plates.

"Oh, how pretty, Mr. Ben!" breathed Caroline.

"Ben?" a woman's voice called from the front of the store.

"That's my Sarah calling, I'm afraid. Let's go find your mother, Caroline."

Caroline took one last look at the china dishes, then followed Mr. Carpenter past barrels of apples and cider to the front of the store. Mother and Mrs. Carpenter were standing at the counter, speaking with Mr. Porter. Henry was there, too, bouncing from foot to foot as he waited for Mother. Caroline chuckled to see his shirt and cheeks streaked with gray from the ashes.

"Looks to me like you were playing in the ashes instead of trading them, young Henry,"

Mr. Carpenter joked. "With any luck all that rain on the horizon will get here just as you're walking home, and you'll not need to worry about washing that shirt."

"Rain?" Mother turned to Mr. Carpenter. "Why, Benjamin, whatever makes you think it will rain? The sun is as bright today as I've ever seen it."

"It's ringed with haze like the head of an angel. No time at all, Charlotte, it'll be raining like water pouring out of a boot." Mr. Carpenter paused and put his cap on his head. "I fear it'll bring wicked winds along with it, too. Might think about pulling all your vegetables. And soon, Charlotte. Shall I come along and help?"

"No, but thank you for the advice. We best be on our way soon." Caroline noticed that Mother's voice was much more cheerful than the look in her eyes.

"Good day, Charlotte, little Brownbraid." Mr. Carpenter winked down at Caroline. "Take good care of your girls," he whispered to Henry. Cupping his wife's elbow, Mr.

Carpenter led her past the men playing checkers near the front of the store. With one last
nod and wave to the Quiners, the Carpenters
were gone.

"I'll be just a minute, children," Mother
said. "I only have a few more things on my
list."

Turning back to the grocer, she said, "I also
need a small packet of tea, Mr. Porter, and
some molasses, please."

Caroline watched as the grocer set the tea on
the counter, and then pried open a big barrel of
molasses. Carefully he lifted a ladle out of the
barrel and slowly poured the thick, dark fluid
into the empty jug Mother had given him.
"Anything else, Mrs. Quiner?" he asked.

"I'd like one paper of sewing needles, and
what's left of that bolt of dark-blue calico
material," Mother answered.

"Are you certain you don't want to take wool
this time of year, Mrs. Quiner?" The grocer
looked at her, one eyebrow raised.

"Mrs. Carpenter just told me what she
paid for wool," Mother answered tartly. "The

cotton will serve my purpose for now."

"All right, then," Mr. Porter said. He searched up and down three rows of shelves that were filled with bolts of material in all colors, fabrics, and prints until he found the material Mother wanted. "Anything else?" he asked.

Caroline edged up to the counter so she could examine the shelves behind the grocer more closely. There were dozens of bolts of colored, dotted, and flowered cotton, wool, and silk, and buttons of all colors, sizes, and shapes were displayed, as were thimbles and needles. Farther along the shelves Caroline spied slates and slate pencils, spelling books, readers, and playing cards. The sweet smell of cinnamon sticks, nutmeg, cloves, and many other spices mingled in the air, making the front of the store smell delicious. Right beside the spices, Caroline spotted dainty soaps and candles, pickles and lemons, even hats and gloves. Caroline gazed at it all in wonder. How could anyone ever decide what to buy?

Ducking around to the other side of Mother,

Caroline squeezed in beside Henry and peered above the counter. One glass jar held tall, thin, red-and-white-striped sticks, while another held little round balls of assorted colors.

"Look, Henry!" Caroline whispered. "Candy!"

"How many pennies do you s'pose we'd need to get one, Caroline?" Henry whispered back.

"That will be all. Thank you, Mr. Porter," Mother said.

Studying the ledger, the grocer said, "I'll credit you for the ashes, Mrs. Quiner, and I'll carry your balance until the next time you're in."

"That will be fine. Thank you again." Mother smiled at the grocer, picked up her basket of goods, and handed Henry the jug of molasses. "Please carry this, Henry-O," she said, turning for the door. "Come now, Caroline."

Caroline followed slowly, drinking in all the sights one more time. Before she stepped out into the sunlight, the crowd of townsfolk, and the cold autumn air, she looked back at the jars filled with candy. Suddenly she knew exactly what she would most like to buy at the grocer's. If only wishes were pennies.

Early Frost

"I saw Mr. Carpenter at the grocer's today," Mother announced that night over the clinking and clanking of supper forks and plates. "He seems to think we're in for some nasty weather."

"How does he know?" Joseph asked in between bites.

"He said he'd been watching the sun all morning, and he noticed that a haze had formed around it," Mother replied as she wiped the sticky sweet potatoes off Thomas's fingers. "He expected we'd see a lot of rain tonight or tomorrow and advised that we finish harvesting the garden as soon as possible. Heavy rains or harsh winds could ruin the crop, and we need to store those vegetables for winter. So early tomorrow morning we must bring in the rest of the vegetables." Mother turned to Grandma. "If you'll watch Eliza and Thomas while the other children and I work in the garden, I would be ever thankful."

"Of course, Charlotte." Grandma nodded. "But are the remaining vegetables ready to be harvested?"

"Not all of them," Mother answered. "It is clearly a risk, Mother Quiner, and I'd give anything to have Henry here to tell us what to do with the rest of the harvest." Mother sighed, and the children looked up at her, surprised. Noticing their concerned faces, Mother softened her voice. "Father is not here, and I have decided that we must pick the remaining crop. It's better to have vegetables that are not yet ripe than no vegetables at all."

The room was silent, and every face was serious as Mother looked around the table. "We must clean the dishes and get to bed right away," Mother said gently. "I'll wake all of you very early."

Martha dropped her fork on her plate, and Caroline noticed a frown darkening her face. Martha hated to get out of bed early any day, and tomorrow they'd have to get up even earlier than usual. Caroline hoped Martha would not complain to Mother. Mother had enough worry on her face and in her voice already, and Martha must not make it worse.

Mother noticed Martha's frown as quickly as Caroline did. "If we're going to get the vegetables picked before the bad weather comes, we'll all need to help, Martha," she said. "We'll have very little food to carry us through the winter if we lose the rest of the crop."

"Yes, ma'am," Martha said contritely, and began nibbling at her dinner again. Mother turned to Caroline. "This will be your first time helping us harvest, Caroline, now, when we especially need your help." Caroline flushed with pleasure, and began to feel a little better.

"Does Mr. Ben think it will only rain,

Mother, or does he fear a very big storm?" Joseph asked.

"Mr. *Carpenter* wasn't certain, Joseph," Mother said pointedly, "but I felt a chill in the air on the way back from town that was cooler than any I've felt yet this fall. I wouldn't be at all surprised if the rain came with a lot of cold wind and turned into a mighty storm."

The room was silent again except for the clinking of forks against plates.

"At least there isn't any wind yet to speak of." Mother's most cheerful voice interrupted the silence. "These windowpanes rattle if one simply whistles in front of them. They will surely warn us if the winds arrive."

Caroline looked down at the round red tomato on her plate. Mother had stuffed it with onions, tomato seeds, stale crumbs of bread, bits of chopped ham, and butter. Earlier that day at dinner, the tomatoes, corn bread, and sweet potatoes were piping hot and delicious. Now, at supper, the leftover tomatoes and their stuffing were cold and much less tasty. But Caroline wasn't thinking about how much better supper had tasted when it was dinner. She wasn't even thinking about the candies that had filled her thoughts ever since she had left the grocer's. All she could think about was the peas, lima beans, and squash still out in the garden, waiting to be picked, and the corn she had been minding for so long. She hoped with all her might that they wouldn't get caught in a terrible storm. They had taken too much work and time to grow.

After supper Caroline and Martha dried the dishes and carefully stacked each one on the dish dresser. Henry refilled the wood box, while Joseph shaved a long stick of cordwood into small bits of wood that Mother could use to make the fire jump and roar again in the morning.

When Joseph had finished whittling the cordwood, he placed it by the hearth and called, "Caroline, come hold the door open while Henry and I get a log for the fire."

"Yes, Joseph."

A few moments after Joseph and Henry left to get the log from the woodpile, Caroline pulled the door open. A sudden blast of cold air struck her face. The cool breeze of the early afternoon had become bitter cold air that rushed through her skirts and shocked her bare legs.

"Move away from that door, Caroline," Mother said, as the cold draft swept across the floor. "Goodness glory, I had no idea how much colder it was getting. I'll hold the door for the boys."

Mother stood in the doorway and waited. When Joseph and Henry returned, she pushed the door shut against the cold air as the boys rolled the heavy log to the hearth. "You boys must be cold clear down to your boots!" Mother exclaimed. "Hurry and set that log in the fire so you can warm yourselves some."

Henry and Joseph hoisted the giant oak log onto the embers. A glowing gold and orange shower of sparks burst from beneath the log and pranced up the chimney. Joseph reached for the iron poker while Henry grabbed a smaller log. Together they shoved the log to the back of the fireplace, where it began to slowly burn. Standing in front of the fire, they rubbed their hands briskly up and down their arms and legs.

"We may need to keep the fire going all night, Mother," Joseph said. "I'll tend it."

"I don't think it's that cold yet, Joseph," Mother said. "Just be certain to put your quilts on your beds. And all of you should wear your flannel nightclothes."

On most nights the children sat around the fire and listened to Mother and Grandma tell stories. Tonight, however, they kissed Grandma, Thomas, and Mother and went quietly upstairs. Caroline could feel the cold air creeping down the stairs from her room, and she shivered, thinking of the cold night and day ahead.

Reaching far into the chest at the foot of the bed, Martha pulled out three flannel night-gowns and caps as Caroline unbuttoned Eliza's dress. Eliza shivered, and her teeth began to chatter as Caroline pulled her dress over her head, quickly replaced it with a flannel night-gown, and buttoned it up the back.

"I'm so cold, Caroline," Eliza whispered, her big eyes welling up with tears.

Caroline tied the strings of Eliza's nightcap securely beneath her chin and pulled the quilt over the bed. "Hurry under the covers, Eliza," Caroline said kindly. "It will be much warmer there." As soon as Eliza was tucked beneath the quilt, Caroline quickly pulled on her own nightgown. The cold draft that had chilled Caroline at the back door and on the stairs was now sweeping across the floor in search of her bare legs. Shivering all over, she brushed her hair and tucked it inside her nightcap as Martha helped fasten the buttons on the back of her nightgown. She jumped under the covers the moment Martha pulled the last loop over its tiny white button.

"How could it ever get so cold so fast?" Martha moaned as she scrambled into bed on the other side of Eliza and pulled the quilt up tightly beneath her chin. "It's too cold, too cold to harvest all those vegetables in the morning."

"What if it rains, too?" Caroline asked in her softest voice. Even though she was snuggled beneath the quilt, the cold had crept into her toes, fingers, and cheeks. She couldn't imagine picking all those ears of corn when she was cold and dry, never mind cold and wet.

"Joseph!" Martha whispered loudly enough for her brother to hear her through the curtain. "If the rains come, will we still bring in all the vegetables in the morning?"

"I don't know," Joseph answered quietly. "Go to sleep, Martha."

"He's only three years older than I am," Martha grumbled to Caroline. "Why does he always have to tell me what to do?"

"Because he's the oldest," Caroline whispered, and she snuggled closer to Eliza.

"I'll never be the oldest," Martha sighed. "I wish I could be the oldest and tell everyone else what to do!"

Caroline didn't say a word. All she wanted was for the cold to go away. She closed her eyes tightly and listened for the awful wind. She was certain that it was seeping through the windowpanes, because she felt it floating above her cheeks. Cold like this had visited many times before, but always after the pumpkins had grown big and turned orange. Many of their pumpkins were still small and green, and Caroline wished as hard as she could that the cold would go away until all the pumpkins were ready to be picked.

Footsteps echoed on the wooden stairs, and Mother was tucking the quilt even tighter around them.

"Did you say your prayers?" she asked softly.

"The floor was so cold, Mother . . ." Martha began.

"You needn't kneel beside the bed tonight." Mother's voice was gentle. "But we must say our prayers."

Caroline, Martha, and Eliza closed their eyes, folded their hands under the quilt, and prayed with Mother. Caroline could just hear Joseph's and Henry's voices joining in from the other side of the room. Though she spoke very softly, Mother's voice was the loudest. When they finished praying, Mother leaned over and kissed each forehead.

"Mother?" Caroline whispered as Mother turned to leave the room.

"What is it?"

"How did our room get so cold so fast?"

"The winds wanted to surprise us, I imagine."

Caroline loved surprises, but not cold surprises like this. "Good night, Mother," she said, and closed her eyes.

"Good night, girls," Mother replied. "Good night, Joseph. Good night, Henry-O."

As Mother disappeared down the stairs, the room grew silent. Caroline heard only Eliza and Martha breathing softly and steadily, and the fingertips of the mighty oak outside their window tap, tap, tapping at the glass panes. The winds must be out there somewhere, Caroline thought. Lying still for many long minutes, she waited. Even if the winds weren't whistling outside the windows or rattling the glass panes, she could still feel them sending cold air all around the room.

Just as Caroline was finally feeling warm and sleepy, the kitchen door slammed below her. Caroline heard Joseph jump out of bed, and she looked at Martha and Eliza. They were still sleeping soundly.

Pushing the covers back, Caroline slid off the bed. Cold air rushed all around her as she tiptoed across the bare wooden floorboards and peeked around the curtain.

"Joseph," Caroline whispered, "what's wrong?"

Joseph turned away from the window, where he stood looking down at the garden. "You should be in bed, Caroline," he chided.

"But the door slammed, and—"

Caroline hadn't even finished her sentence when Henry bounded out of bed. "What's going on?" he asked, stifling a yawn.

"It's Mother," Joseph answered, pointing to the window. "She's out in the garden."

Caroline followed Henry to the window and squeezed between her two brothers so she could see outside. Pressing her face right up to the glass pane, she stared out at the darkness. A yellow light was flickering in the garden. Between the thick branches and trembling leaves of the old oak that stood beside the window, Caroline could see someone kneeling in the dirt.

"Is that Mother?" Caroline asked, her voice hushed.

"Yes," said Joseph. "She must be picking the vegetables."

"She *is* picking them," Henry said. "Look. There's a basket next to her."

Silence hung between them as they watched Mother hurry from ground to basket and back again. Before Father had gone away, Mother had never worked in the garden. Now she was alone in the dark and the bitter cold, trying to save as many vegetables as she could. Caroline felt a lump in her throat, and tears pricked her eyes.

"How long do you think that torch will burn?" Henry asked Joseph as he studied the light flickering in the garden.

"It looks very tall. If it's an old broom handle, it should burn for a while," Joseph answered.

The heavens disagreed. A torrent suddenly burst from the skies, and angry raindrops pelted the windowpanes as Caroline, Joseph, and Henry stood horrified and watched the light in the garden flicker out.

"We must go help!" Caroline urged. "We can't leave Mother alone in the rain and cold!"

"I'm going, Caroline," Joseph said in his most Father-like voice. "Get back to bed before you catch your death in this cold. Henry, mind the house while I'm gone."

For the first time in months, Henry didn't tease Joseph about acting so big. He and Caroline hurried back to bed. Caroline was careful not to awaken Martha or Eliza, though both stirred as she climbed back under the quilt and moved closer to their warm bodies. Settling her capped head on the pillow, she listened to the rain pounding the roof and waited for the kitchen door to open and close again. Why was Mother out in the garden picking vegetables when they had planned to harvest in the morning? Caroline had never heard of anyone gathering a crop after bedtime. And she was sure that Mother would never have set an old broomstick on fire unless it was very, very important. It was far too dangerous.

What would Mother do without the light from the torch to help her see all the vegetables that needed to be picked? Which vegetables would she pick? Which would she leave behind to brave the cold and the rain?

It was impossible now for Caroline to sleep when she had so many questions. She closed her eyes tightly and fought hard not to think about the biggest question of all: What would they eat all winter if the cold took their vegetables?

Pumpkin Pickles

"Wake up, girls."

Caroline opened her eyes and saw Mother's gray wool dress with the little white buttons that climbed all the way up to her chin. Her hair was already neatly tucked beneath her bonnet, and she looked weary.

Caroline's nose and toes and fingers ached with cold, and suddenly she remembered the garden. Mother was supposed to wake them before the sun rose so they could pick the vegetables. But the room was already bright with daylight. Mother had not awakened them early.

"Are we going to pick the vegetables now, Mother?" Caroline asked.

Mother's eyes were grave. "No, Caroline. I picked as many as I could last night. The rest will have to stay out in the garden."

Martha opened her eyes and sat straight up in bed.

"It's already morning, Mother! We must go to the garden!" she exclaimed, rubbing the sleep out of her eyes.

"It is time to get out of bed," Mother answered, "but we'll not be going to the garden."

Caroline suddenly felt the frigid air outside the quilt. Hastily she pulled the covers up beneath her chin. "I thought we were going to pick all the vegetables today!" she cried. "Remember? You said that I could help pick them this year!"

Sitting down beside Caroline, Mother hugged her. "The vegetables in the garden are even colder this morning than we are. They had to stay outside all night."

"So we can't pick them, Mother? We can't eat them?" Martha asked.

"No, Martha." Mother was solemn. "I'm afraid that the vegetables are no longer good to eat."

"Won't we even be able to eat the vegetables that you and I picked last night, Mother?" Joseph asked.

Caroline was so shocked by the awful words Mother was saying that she hadn't even heard Joseph get out of bed. He was standing in front of them, his forehead wrinkled with worry.

"Of course we will, Joseph," Mother said firmly. "We should be able to eat most everything we picked before the frost settled completely last night. That food should hold out for a while. And of course, we have all the potatoes, turnips, beets, and onions that are still under the dirt, protected from the frost. We have yet to pick any of them." Mother stood up and smiled cheerfully. "Don't worry, children, we'll have plenty of good food to eat. If it warms up this morning, we'll all go out into the garden and see what's left. Perhaps we didn't lose so much to the frost after all. Now, all of you, out of bed. Breakfast is waiting, and the day is wasting!" On her way down the stairs, she added, "Make certain that you dress quickly, children, and that you wear your flannels. The fire in the hearth hasn't yet had time enough to warm this room."

"I'll get our clothes, Caroline," Martha said. "You and Eliza stay under the quilt." Caroline nodded. She was happy to stay under the warm quilt for another moment or two. Martha snatched three sets of flannels, wool dresses, aprons, stockings, and shoes from the chest, and tossed them over to the bed.

"Stay under the covers 'til we finish, Eliza," Caroline ordered. The cold air nipped her fingers and toes as she slid out of bed. Caroline quickly pulled her nightgown off, and her flannels on. Before she even had time to raise her dress over her head, the flannel began scratching her skin.

Martha was pulling on her shoes as Caroline asked, "Do you think it's worse to be full of itches, or full of cold?"

"It's worst of all to have shoes that pinch your toes! Ouch!" Martha groaned as she forced her stockinged toes into her shoe.

As Martha dressed Eliza, Caroline glanced around the room. Something was strange. Every morning when the sun's golden beams came floating through the windowpanes, the little room glowed. But this morning, the room was filled from floor to rafters with a hazy white light, and the windows weren't letting any golden beams through their glass panes.

Caroline looked more closely at the windowpane. "Oh, Martha!" she marveled. "Come look!" The glass was covered by thick white frost, its swirls and diamonds and snowflake patterns delicately dusted all over the window. Caroline gently touched the bottom corner of the windowpane with one fingertip, and the frost began to melt. Lining her eye up with the tiny clear circle, Caroline peeked outside.

The sun was shining brilliantly from a glassy blue sky. Wanting to see more, Caroline cleared one big circle in the middle of the windowpane with her warm hand. Then she looked back out on the dazzling world of white. Beneath her little room, the pines and maples, the barn, the roof of the henhouse, the split logs in the wood-pile, the corn and squash and tomatoes in the garden rested silently beneath their icy white blankets. Most of the leaves of the great oak that grew outside her window had disappeared overnight, leaving the bare branches trembling beneath a pebbly cover of ice and frost.

Martha squeezed in next to Caroline and looked outside. "It looks so cold," she exclaimed.

"I want to see! I want to see!" Eliza jumped up and down on the floor behind them, eager for a glimpse.

Caroline hoisted Eliza up. "Pretty!" Eliza said, and pressed her little nose against the window. "Cold!" she wailed, and buried her face in Caroline's shoulder. Caroline looked over Eliza's head at Martha and giggled.

"Girls!" The sound of Mother's voice sent all three sisters running down the stairs to breakfast. Joseph and Henry had already finished carrying in wood for the fire and filling the washbasin with fresh water. Grandma and Mother had set the table and gathered all the chairs. The roaring fire in the hearth made the room feel warm and cozy, and the sweet smell of toasted bread filled the house. Mother placed a piece of toast on each plate and poured a steaming hot sauce made of milk, butter, and flour all over the browned slices of bread. As she dug into her breakfast, the hot milk-toast warmed Caroline all the way down to her toes.

Mother didn't speak until breakfast was nearly finished. Then she said, "We'll do the dishes now, children, but we'll leave the rest of our morning chores until we find out if there are any vegetables that survived the frost in the garden."

As soon as the last dish was dried and back on the dish dresser, Caroline wrapped her shawl snugly around her head and shoulders and followed Mother outside. The cold air stung her cheeks and filled her lungs, and the sharp glare of the sun on the frozen white land-scape brought tears to the corners of her eyes. The world was strangely silent, as if all the birds and tiny animals that chirped and sang and squawked in it had run away to hide.

Picking her way carefully through the frosted grass, Caroline followed Mother to the garden that only yesterday had been a vibrant field of colors. The frozen, droopy tangle of tomato vines looked more black than green, and dozens of pale orange tomatoes littered the ground. The squash and the pumpkins, just beginning to turn from green to yellow and orange, were thickly covered with frost. Caroline's heart sank as she looked at the once proud stalks of corn hunched over beneath the weight of the thick white frost. Despite their bright colors and glittering white coats, the vegetables looked limp and lifeless. The frost that had seemed so beautiful to Caroline from the upstairs bedroom now seemed anything but beautiful. It had killed their vegetables before they had ever had a chance to finish growing.

Caroline knelt beside a frozen vine and cradled a tiny round tomato in her hand. "Can we still pick them, Mother?" she asked.

"We should pick some of them," Mother

answered soberly. And then, more firmly, she announced, "No! We will pick every vegetable we can find, children. Whatever a man soweth, so shall he reap. We worked too hard to keep these plants growing, and we will find *something* to do with every one of these vegetables. Joseph and Henry, bring every basket and pail that you can find out of the barn."

Mother's words cheered everyone, and they all bustled about, almost forgetting the cold as their fingers flew across the droopy vines and plants.

By the time every basket, crate, and pail was filled with vegetables, the warm sun was fixed at the very top of the sky. The frost began to melt and drip to the earth from the leaves and branches where it nestled. All the color had now been picked from the garden; only an ugly darkening green remained in the wilted vines, leaves, and stalks.

As dinnertime neared, Henry asked, "Are we also going to pick the potatoes and turnips today, Mother?"

Looking up from the gnarled vine she was

pulling out of the ground, Mother answered, "We'll pull some of the root vegetables after dinner, Henry-O, but not all. This frost killed the garden, but the ground is still warm. One frost won't freeze it for good. The plants beneath the earth should continue to grow safely for a little while longer." Mother straightened up, shading her eyes with her hand, as she looked at the sky. "The only clouds I see are high in the sky," she said. "I'm certain that means we're in for some good weather. We'll eat dinner now, and afterward, Caroline can help you and Joseph dig some of the potatoes while Martha, Grandma, and I prepare the ripe tomatoes we picked for preserves."

Caroline silently looked down at the cold, wet earth and the piles of dead vines and plants. She was glad that the root vegetables were safe underground, but she wished that she could help Mother make preserves instead of digging for potatoes. Today was the first time she had ever helped harvest. Her back ached from bending over the frozen vines, and her arms hurt from picking so many squashes and tomatoes. Looking down at her hands, she tried to wipe away some of the green and brown stains, but they wouldn't disappear, no matter how hard she rubbed. Her fingers were stiff and cold, and once she began digging potatoes from the ground, they'd be caked with the soggy dirt, too. She had badly stained the only apron that still fit her by kneeling on the wet ground. The shoes that she had tried so hard to keep clean were wet and covered with thick, sticky mud. All this misery from one terrible frost.

Caroline felt like crying as she trudged back to the house. Then she thought about Mother, who had been outside all night in the rain and cold. She had enough to worry about. Caroline didn't want to cry or complain to her about going back to the garden.

Grandma greeted them with baked beans for dinner, and for a moment Caroline forgot about her apron and shoes as she ate her beans and corn bread and drank her milk. After everyone had been eating ravenously for a few minutes, Martha spoke up. "What will we do with the all the vegetables that are not yet ripe, Mother?"

"We'll wash and peel them, Martha," Mother answered, "and after we finish slicing them, we'll cook them with vinegar and spices, and some salt and pepper. We may not be able to eat them as they are, but we'll be able to have tomato, squash, and pumpkin pickles all winter!"

"Pumpkin pickles!" Henry cried. "Who ever heard of pumpkin pickles?"

"No one yet, Henry-O," Mother admitted. "Now you and Joseph hurry out to the garden, and please start carrying in the vegetables we picked. As soon as we finish the dishes, I'll send Caroline to help you dig up some of the rest."

"Oh, Mother," Martha blurted out, "couldn't I help Joseph and Henry? Couldn't Caroline stay here with you and Grandma and help with the preserves? I'll dig as fast as I can, and I'll come back and help you with the preserves in no time."

Caroline looked up, her eyes full of hope. Mother looked from Martha to Caroline and then back again. "You are the fastest picker, Martha, after all," she said. "The boys could certainly use your help. But I expect you to return as soon as you fill one bushel basket with potatoes. Henry-O and Joseph can dig up the rest."

"Yes, ma'am," Martha crowed, and she clapped her hands. Caroline clapped too, her eyes dancing.

"You'd best finish your dinner, Caroline," Mother added. "We've plenty of pickling to do."

Picking up her fork, Caroline smiled at Mother and quickly finished the beans on her plate. No more digging, and she could help Mother and Grandma make pumpkin pickles. The cold, terrible frost hadn't ruined everything after all.

Two Birthdays

Drifts of snow hugged the rooftop of the frame house, and frost covered the windowpanes. Winter had come to Brookfield.

The last potatoes, turnips, carrots, and beets had been pulled from the ground and stored safely in the root cellar beneath the kitchen. Jars of pickles and preserves lined the pantry shelves. Whenever Caroline went into the pantry to fetch something for Mother, she tried hard to admire the hard-won stock of vegetables, and not to look at the nearly empty barrels of dried fish, or the empty rafters that had once hung thick with dried meat when Father was here.

"Terrible cold!" Joseph rushed through the kitchen door and slammed it shut against the winds that swirled in a fury outside. He stamped his feet at the door, and snowflakes tumbled from his shoulders to the plank floor below as he hurried to drop his armful of logs into the wood box.

"Joseph, make certain that you clear up that floor," Mother said without even looking up from the gray flannel shirt she was mending.

"Yes, ma'am," Joseph answered.

The flames in the hearth leaped and danced as Caroline sat sewing on her sampler. Her stomach grumbled with hunger, even though she and Martha had just finished putting away the supper dishes. Tonight they had eaten only the little bit of fish and potatoes left from the dinner they'd had earlier that day. Closing her eyes for a moment, Caroline tried to imagine the smell of hot, fresh bread, but all she could smell was the warm, smoky aroma of burning wood that always filled the room. Feeling even hungrier, she looked over at Grandma, who was knitting in the rocker beside her.

"Grandma," Caroline asked, "could you please help me finish this stitch?"

"Why, of course, dear. Come. Sit up here," Grandma said, helping Caroline onto her lap.

Grandma examined Caroline's sampler and whispered into her ear, "Your work is lovely." She covered Caroline's hands with her own, and together they began pulling the needle through the stiff cloth while Caroline watched closely.

"All finished!" Henry shouted, and jumped up from the floor where he had been sitting cross-legged. He carried the handful of shavings he had whittled to Mother. "I've enough to stoke the fire come morning. All right if we play checkers now?"

Mother looked past her needle and thread at Henry's outstretched hands and nodded. "Thank you, Henry-O. Yes, you may play checkers."

Caroline looked up from her sewing as Henry dropped his shavings in the tinder box by the hearth and Joseph pulled out their

homemade checkerboard and corncob checkers and set them on the floor. She loved watching her brothers play checkers. They always sat
on the floor in front of the fire and played quietly until Henry jumped one of Joseph's
checkers. Scooping up the corncob checker
he'd just jumped, Henry would shout,
"Whoop! Beat you at that one, Joseph!" and
slam it on the floor next to his side of the
board. Mother would shake her head and
admonish him—"Henry-O, he who knows
how to keep silent knows a great deal!"—
while Joseph quietly stewed. Caroline felt a little bit sorry for Joseph, because Henry was a
much better checkers player. But she still loved
it when Henry jumped his checkers, because
Henry's "Whoop!" always made her want to
laugh out loud.

The fire hissed and popped, and tree
branches tapped at the windowpanes as
Caroline and Martha sewed, and Mother softly
sang and mended. Though Caroline was looking down at her sampler, she listened intently
to every word that Mother sang.

"Green grows the laurel, and so does the rue;
So woeful my love, at the parting with you.
But by our next meeting our love we'll renew;
We'll change the green laurel to the orange
and blue."

Caroline knew each word of Mother's song by heart, because Mother had been singing the very same song ever since Father had gone away on his schooner. Sometimes Caroline wondered what a laurel and a rue were, and how the laurel could change from green to orange and blue. But she never interrupted Mother to ask.

Mother hummed the melody of the song, and Caroline remembered how Father used to wait every evening until Mother began sewing. Even before Mother was settled in her rocker, Father would whisk Caroline and Martha up onto his lap and say, "Sing now, Charlotte! We've all waited too long!" Mother's singing would fill the room, and Father would close his eyes and listen. It wasn't until she finished the last note that he'd look up at the rafters and whisper, "Heavenly! Like listening to the angels, your mother when she sings!"

"Whoop! Beat you at that one, Joseph!" Henry shouted gleefully.

Mother stopped humming and looked sternly at Henry. "Henry-O," she warned, "he who knows how to keep silent knows a great deal."

"Yes, Mother." Henry tried to hide the wide grin on his face as Caroline pressed her hands to her mouth to stifle her own giggles.

"Could you sing another song, now, Mother? A faster one?" Martha pleaded. Martha didn't like slow songs, especially the song about the laurels. She always wanted to dance, and she liked it best when Mother's singing was bright and lively.

"What song would you like?" Mother asked.

"I want to polly-wolly-doodle all the day!" Martha cried.

Mother smiled, her eyes crinkling up at the corners. Setting the gray shirt she was mending on her lap, she began clapping and merrily singing:

Two Birthdays

"Oh, I went down south for to see my Sal,
Sing polly-wolly-doodle all the day;
My Sally was a spunky gal,
Sing polly-wolly-doodle all the day.
Farewell, farewell, farewell, my fairy fay,
For I'm off to Louisiana
For to see my Susy Anna,
Singing polly-wolly-doodle all the day."

Skirts and braids swinging back and forth, Martha clapped and danced in front of the hearth. Grandma helped Caroline tie up the last strand of thread on her sampler, and Caroline slid down from her lap and spun around and around on the floor as she clapped and sang along with Mother and Martha. Mother's voice was bright, but she didn't jump from her chair and dance with Martha and Caroline as she used to when Father was home. She simply finished her song, picked up her mending, and crossed over to the sewing table. "I must work on Mrs. Stoddard's dress if I am to finish it in time for Christmas," she said. Mrs. Stoddard lived next door to the Quiners in one of the grandest houses in Brookfield, and Caroline thought the lovely dresses that Mother made for her were the most beautiful clothes in the world.

"May I watch?" Caroline asked eagerly as Mother tucked the shirt in a basket and spread long layers of dark-green crinkly material over the sewing table.

"Have you finished another letter, Caroline?" Mother asked.

"Yes, Mother," Caroline answered.

"Then you may watch."

Caroline had never seen such beautiful material. The dark-green cloth flowed down the table all the way to the floor. It was so richly colored, it looked almost too exquisite to touch.

"Where did such pretty material come from, Mother?" Caroline asked.

"Mrs. Stoddard had it sent from back East," Mother replied. Her nimble fingers pushed the needle and thread back and forth through the material so quickly that Caroline could barely follow them. Certainly no one could sew faster or better than Mother, Caroline thought. Before she met Father, Mother had her own dress shop in Boston. Soon after Father went to heaven and Grandma came to live with them, Mother began mending and making dresses and shirts again. Caroline had watched Mother make elegant dresses out of nothing but plain cloth before, and she couldn't wait to see how this precious material would look once Mother's fingers and thread transformed it into a dress.

"When will Mrs. Stoddard wear such a pretty dress?" Martha asked from behind Caroline.

"For Christmas," Mother said.

Caroline and Martha looked at each other, their eyes glowing. "Christmas!" Martha exclaimed. "How soon until Christmas?"

"Just a few more weeks." Mother smiled. "A few weeks after Caroline's birthday."

"Henry and Joseph!" Martha interrupted their game of checkers. "It's almost Christmas!"

"When will my birthday be, Mother?" Caroline asked.

"I believe it's in four more days, Caroline," Mother said as she counted silently to herself. "Yes. Just four more days."

"But I thought I didn't have a birthday," Caroline said hesitantly.

Mother looked up abruptly from the dark-green cloth. "Why, of course you do. Whatever makes you think that you do not?" she asked.

Caroline had often wondered how she had turned five without a birthday, but she had never asked Mother. Now was her chance. Martha had birthdays, and so did Joseph and Henry. Even Thomas and Eliza had birthdays. Caroline wanted to have a birthday, too.

Glancing up from her needlework, Grandma spoke softly to Mother. "We didn't celebrate Caroline's birthday last year, Charlotte. Elisha and Margaret and I had just arrived with the news."

Mother's face fell, and Caroline wished that Grandma had never said those words, even if it meant that she would never have another birthday. All of a sudden Caroline remembered Mother saying, "Father will be home any day now, children. As soon as the schooner comes back to port." But instead, Uncle Elisha, Aunt Margaret, and Grandma had arrived from the big city of Milwaukee. Mother left the house to greet them as Caroline, her brothers, and Martha watched from the window in the parlor.

Closing her eyes tightly, Caroline tried to forget seeing Uncle Elisha help Grandma and Aunt Margaret out of the wagon. They were all dressed in black. Aunt Margaret clutched a white handkerchief, and she wiped away the tears that streamed down her cheeks. Uncle Elisha looked at the ground and scuffed the toe of his black boot in the dirt. When he finally looked up, Caroline saw that his eyes were red and puffy. Grandma's face was hidden by a long black veil, and Uncle Elisha had his arm tucked solidly beneath hers. "Something is wrong," Joseph had said. No one spoke or moved. They all just watched as Mother buried her face in her hands, and Aunt Margaret hugged her. Grandma, Uncle Elisha, and Aunt Margaret had come that day to tell them that Father's schooner had been lost in a terrible storm. Uncle Elisha and Aunt Margaret stayed in the frame house for many, many days, until Mother felt better, and Grandma had lived with them ever since. Father had never returned.

"I remember now," Mother said. Kneeling down in front of Caroline, Mother looked into her eyes. "We didn't celebrate your birthday last year because we were all too sad for a celebration. But this year we aren't sad, Caroline. This year you will have your birthday. As a matter of fact"—she clapped her hands— "we'll celebrate two birthdays. Five *and* six!"

Mother's merriness made Caroline instantly forget that she was sad and hungry. Suddenly she was in a terrible hurry to get to bed so that she could help the days go by faster. Running up the stairs after Martha, she could think of nothing else. Two birthdays! Caroline had never before heard of anyone who celebrated two birthdays on the very same day. Hardly noticing the chill in the room, she pulled on her nightgown, tucked her hair inside her cap, and climbed in under the covers. Only four more days!

It seemed to Caroline that the next three days lasted a whole week, so slowly did they pass. The morning light hadn't even made its way into the bedroom when Caroline opened her eyes on the fourth day. The room was silent as she crept out of bed and dressed so quietly that she didn't wake anyone. She brushed her hair until it shone and tiptoed downstairs with her blue ribbon. Grandma and Mother were just beginning to prepare breakfast.

"My goodness, Caroline!" Mother exclaimed when she saw her. "It is very early for you to be up! Today must be a very special day!"

"Yes, Mother," Caroline answered shyly. She hoped it was still her birthday.

"Hurry and wash your hands and face. The washbasin is not yet filled, but you can use the fresh water that I have in that bucket over there."

Mother nodded toward the kitchen door, and

Caroline knelt down and washed her face and hands, taking care not to soak the ends of her sleeves as she scooped the cold water into her hands.

The juicy smell of frying fat began to fill the kitchen, and Caroline suddenly felt hungry. "Are you making hotcakes, Mother?" she asked hopefully.

"Why, of course, Caroline. Today we're celebrating two birthdays!" Mother's smile spread from one side of her face to the other. "Come, let's braid your hair and get you ready for your special day."

Caroline held her blue ribbon out to Grandma, but Mother said quickly, "I'll braid your hair today, Caroline. Will you please finish stirring this, Mother Quiner?" Handing the bowl and spoon to Grandma, Mother sat on a chair behind Caroline and began twisting and pulling her hair into one long brown braid.

As Mother's nimble fingers neared the bottom of her braid, Caroline handed her the blue ribbon.

"Oh, Caroline," Mother said, "you cannot

wear such an old ribbon on your birthday! You
need something bright and new to begin a new
year!"

Mother spun Caroline around. Catching her
breath, Caroline looked down at the dark-
green ribbon that was lying in Mother's open
hands. The ribbon was made of the same soft
cloth as Mrs. Stoddard's dress, and it was as
lovely as it was new.

"Oh, Mother." Caroline could barely speak.
"It's so beautiful."

"Happy birthday number five!" Mother
laughed and tied the ribbon in a smart bow
around the bottom of Caroline's braid.

Caroline was busy admiring her new ribbon
when Mother reached inside her apron pocket
and pulled out a small bundle that was wrapped
in a swatch of tan cloth. "Happy birthday number six, Caroline," she said, her eyes twinkling.

Caroline gently unfolded the cloth. Hidden
beneath, she found a cheery rag doll's face
smiling up at her. Black button eyes sparkled
in the early-morning light, and curly black yarn
hair was braided from the rag doll's round head

all the way down her plaid dress, where it was tied at the bottom with a tiny, dark-green bow. Caroline lovingly smoothed the doll's dress and touched her bow, which perfectly matched Caroline's brand-new bow.

"Oh, Mother," Caroline whispered, and she pressed her rag doll's little face against her cheek. "My very own doll! I shall call her Abigail!"

"Grandma helped make Abigail," Mother said. "You must thank her, also."

Caroline hurried to hug Grandma as Mother said, "And now I must wake your brothers and sisters so that we can all celebrate together."

Soon the whole family was gathered around the table in the warm, sunny kitchen, feasting on hotcakes and dried apples. They had never had such a merry breakfast! No one even noticed that the hotcakes were made of cornmeal, or that there was no butter or syrup to spread on them.

Caroline held Abigail tightly with one hand and kept reaching behind her back with the other. She wanted to be certain that her

precious bow was still safely wrapped around
the bottom of her braid. Only a few short days
ago she didn't think she had a birthday. Today
she was having not just one birthday, but two.
And the best presents that she could have ever
imagined.

A Stranger's Gift

In the days that followed Caroline's birthday, the bitter December wind decided to stir up trouble in town, and there was no stopping it. Giant swirls of dust, dirt, and broken branches whipped from building to building, and angry winds swiftly pushed brooding dark clouds across the troubled sky.

Mother hurried across the street, her heavy shawl and black wool skirt belling out behind her. Joseph hugged his coat to his chest with one hand and clutched a half dozen rabbit and beaver pelts in the other. Ducking their heads behind Mother and Joseph, Caroline and

Henry followed closely and hid from the wind and dirt that stung their faces.

Caroline almost wished that she had stayed home. She usually loved going to town, but not on such a stormy day. When they finally reached the grocer's, she was happy to leave the windy street behind.

"Now wait here while I speak with Mr. Porter," Mother said to Caroline and her brothers.

"Yes, ma'am."

Mother walked to the front counter, where Mr. Porter was talking to a very tall man. Caroline had always thought Mr. Porter was tall, but the man he was talking to was even taller. The man wore a heavy coat patched together with black, brown, and gray furs. His boots were shiny and black. The brown fur cap that covered his head had a thick black stripe down the middle, and his stubbly beard matched the yellow hair poking out from beneath his cap. Every time he moved his head, his cap bumped the three tin pans hanging from twine above him.

As Mother neared, the very tall man shook Mr. Porter's hand and turned to leave. Henry and Joseph tilted their heads backward as he passed, but he didn't notice them. Instead, the tall man glanced down at Caroline. His dark eyes might have frightened her had they not been accompanied by a gentle smile and a friendly wink. Then he was gone, ducking through the doorway and out into the wind.

"Well, I'll be washed and hung out to dry!" Joseph whispered as the door banged shut. "Did you ever see a man so tall?"

Henry's mouth was still hanging open. "Not ever!"

"I bet when he goes hunting, all the wild animals run away," Caroline chimed in.

"I bet he lives in the woods and gets his head stuck in the branches of trees when he's looking for squirrels and birds to eat. I bet he can tear a big old bear right apart, straight from head to toes!" Henry cried gleefully. "I bet he's a mean, wild man who lives with the bears and eats one or two whenever he gets hungry!"

Caroline jumped as Mother marched up

behind Henry and grabbed his shoulder. "That's quite enough, Henry-O. Shame on you for inventing such stories!"

"But Mother, did you see how tall and terrible he was?" Henry's words spilled out of his mouth, but a stern look from Mother immediately halted them.

"Judge not lest ye be judged, Henry-O," she said. "We don't know anything about that man, and we musn't make up stories. Now pull your cap back over your head. Mr. Porter is out of flour, so we must walk over to the mill and see if Mr. Leavenworth has any to spare."

Caroline tucked her bow and braid up next to her ear and wrapped her shawl tightly around her head and shoulders. She slipped her hand into Mother's. Suddenly she was delighted that she had come along to town. Mother was taking them to the mill!

Great tumbling balls of dust whipped like wheels down the road as the Quiners headed past the edge of town, where it was still mostly forest. The mill stood tall before them. It was dotted with windows on all four sides. The back of the mill stood at the creek's edge, its huge waterwheel hugging its frame. A soaking white spray flew off the paddles of the water-wheel as it turned and churned and whipped even more white foam and bubbles into the swollen creek roaring around it. Caroline knew that the wheel turned huge stones inside the mill, and the stones ground wheat to make flour. Father had told her so.

"May we please go and watch the wheel for a while, Mother?" Henry called out above the howling wind.

"Not today, Henry. No animal should be outside in this wind, much less youngsters like you. It seems to get worse every minute."

Mother hustled Caroline, Henry, and Joseph to the front of the mill. She struggled to open the door, and the wind finally pushed them inside. The whole mill shook and groaned and rattled as though it were having a fit.

"I'll never quite get used to the noise that a waterwheel can make," Mother said loudly as she looked around for the miller. "There's Mr. Leavenworth. Henry-O, wait with Caroline while I speak with him. Joseph, come with me, please."

Caroline and Henry stood still for a moment after Mother and Joseph left. Then Henry said in a hushed voice, "Come on, Caroline. Let's go see what there is to see."

Caroline had heard Mother tell them to wait, but Mother had never said they couldn't walk around the mill. Quickly loosening the shawl from her head, Caroline followed Henry past a great tower of wooden crates and barrels stacked high against one far wall. Tiny kernels of grain crackled beneath her shoes, and the dusty smell of the mill tickled the inside of her nose. She felt like sneezing and giggling at the same time.

All around the stubbly floor, huge piles of grain stood like golden pyramids. Henry reached into the side of one of them, pulled out a handful of grain, and watched as dozens of kernels tumbled swiftly down the side to fill up the hole.

"Do you think we could ever climb one of these, Henry?" Caroline asked, looking high above her brother to the top of the pile.

Each time they came to the mill, she wished she could climb up a pile of grain and touch the ceiling right before she slipped down the other side of the pile and skidded to the floor in a rush of barley, corn, oats, or wheat. But Mother always said that children shouldn't touch the grain or run in the mill if they wanted to visit again. The shovels, rakes, and broomsticks that leaned against the walls might fall and hurt little girls. And Caroline wanted to visit again.

"Not a chance, little Brownbraid," Henry replied. "All this grain would just crumble underneath our toes with every step we took. We'd never get anywhere."

"Maybe we could go watch the creek then," Caroline suggested.

"Let's go!"

Henry grabbed Caroline's hand and pulled her over to the back of the mill, where two long windows looked out over the waterwheel. Standing on her tiptoes, her nose against the glass, Caroline watched the water flip off the paddles of the waterwheel and hurtle down to the creek that dipped and tumbled as it rushed by in a foamy fury. Once she had asked Father why the water rushed by so fast. Father had said that the creek had many different places to visit, and it was in a hurry to see every one. Caroline wondered where the creek was going today.

"I plan to leave this here evening, Leavenworth, should the weather allow. If the winds settle some, I'll be in Milwaukee by morning."

The deep voice startled Caroline, and she spun away from the window. The miller, Mr. Leavenworth, was talking to the tall man they had just seen at the general store. The tall man was going to Milwaukee, a place that Father had often talked about and visited.

"Look, Caroline," Henry whispered from behind her. "It's the man who lives with the bears!"

"I saw him already," Caroline whispered back.

"Come here," Henry said, pulling her out of sight behind a barrel. "Let's listen."

Before either man had a chance to continue speaking, Mother walked up to them. Mr. Leavenworth immediately nodded to her and said, "G'd afternoon, Mrs. Quiner. Be right with you."

The tall man looked down at Mother and Joseph. "I'm in no hurry," he said. "Help the lady first."

"Thank you," Mother said.

The miller caught up one curly end of his black mustache and began twirling it between his fingers. "Well then, how are you and the children today, Mrs. Quiner?" he asked.

"Fine, thank you," Mother answered politely. "But I'm afraid we've used every last bit of flour that we had in the house."

"I've only a couple barrels left." Mr. Leavenworth released his mustache and waved toward the back wall. "Good thing you arrived early, Mrs. Quiner. Both barrels'll be gone before evenin', no doubt. And what with Christmas tomorrow, I don't expect to be milling anymore wheat 'til week's end."

Caroline caught her breath. Christmas! she

remembered. Before Caroline had celebrated her birthdays, Mother had told Martha that Christmas was just a few weeks away. Mother must be planning to make her special Christmas bread.

"Yes, Joseph and I discovered those barrels a moment ago," Mother said. She glanced again at the two large barrels standing against the wall, surrounded by piles of burlap sacks, wooden crates, and empty buckets. "Could we possibly take along just a small sack of flour, Mr. Leavenworth?" Mother asked. "We've brought some rabbit and beaver pelts for trade. Surely they're worth a small sack of flour." Caroline and Henry watched silently from behind their barrel as Joseph proudly held up the pelts that he and Henry had caught.

"Hmmm." Mr. Leavenworth rubbed his big hand over his face and shook his head. "I'm terrible sorry, Mrs. Quiner," he said, "but I only have those two barrels of flour left. I've promised one to Mrs. Wedge, and she's sending Mr. Wedge over to get it 'fore dark. If I break into that last barrel, I may not sell it at all. Most folks want the whole barrel. In two or three days, I'll likely have some left from a new run, and I'll be happy to trade for it then." Mr. Leavenworth turned to Joseph, unable to look at Mother any longer. "Those look like fine pelts, son. You hold on to them for me one or two more days, hear?"

Mother put her hand on Joseph's arm. The smile on her lips and in her eyes had disappeared. "Let's find your brother and sister, Joseph," she said, and added, "Thank you for your time, Mr. Leavenworth. We will return at the end of the week."

"Wait just a minute, Mrs. Quiner." Mr. Leavenworth's eyes brightened, and he hurried toward his front counter. "I've got me an idea!"

As Mother and Joseph followed Mr. Leavenworth across the dusty floor, Henry grabbed Caroline's arm. "Hurry, Caroline," he said, "let's get back up front!"

Reaching the door just before Mother and Joseph, Caroline and Henry watched as Mr. Leavenworth pulled a small burlap sack from beneath a stool.

"Someone brought this bit of brown sugar to me just yesterday, but I have no need for it. You're certain to put it to better use than I." Holding the bag out, he added, "I know it isn't much, but it's something."

Mother did not take the bag. "Thank you," she said politely, "but it's the flour we need. Good day to you." Turning around, she looked for Henry and Caroline.

"There you are!" she said. "Mr. Leavenworth won't be milling wheat today, so we'll have to wait a day or two before we can take some flour home."

"When is Christmas, Mother?" Caroline asked.

"Tomorrow, Caroline."

Henry was suddenly thinking about Mother's Christmas bread, too. "How will you make your Christmas bread without any flour?" he asked.

"We'll make a special corn bread instead, Henry," Mother answered, and turned to Caroline. "Don't look so sad, Caroline. We will have a fine Christmas dinner. There will be corn bread and gravy, potatoes and turnips, and in a few days, we'll have the whole house smelling like fresh bread again."

Caroline tried to smile back at Mother, but inside she did not feel like smiling at all. She hated to go home without any flour, or to have Christmas come and go without Mother's special sweet bread. She wanted to open one of those barrels and fill an empty sack with flour until it was bulging from side to side and was taller and fatter than Joseph. It wouldn't even matter if she ended up covered with flour from her new ribbon down to her shoes. Joseph and Henry could carry the sack home. Mother would be so happy, and they wouldn't have to wait any more days for fresh bread.

"Can we take the brown sugar along with us, Mother?" Caroline asked, wondering why Mother hadn't taken the small sack from Mr. Leavenworth. Caroline would have said, "Thank you, sir," and run all the way home with it. Then as soon as they had more flour, Mother could make her very special sweet bread and Grandma could make her sweet cakes.

"No, Caroline," Mother's voice was firm. "We didn't come to the mill for brown sugar. We came for flour, and we cannot get any today." Reaching down, Mother pulled Caroline's shawl back over and around her head and tucked the corners beneath her arms. "Now let's be on our way. Grandma is keeping dinner for us."

Knowing that she shouldn't bother Mother anymore, Caroline kept all her questions inside. She glanced once more at the burlap sack Mr. Leavenworth still held in his big hand, and found the tall man looking over at her again with his dark eyes; only this time he wasn't smiling. His eyes looked as sad as Caroline felt.

Leading the way through the town, Joseph and Henry ducked their heads against the wind, which had grown even angrier during their brief visit to the mill. A stinging gray cloud of dust and dirt whirled furiously around them, making it hard to see the road. Caroline held Mother's hand tightly and kicked at the sticks and twigs that flew at her and got tangled in her skirt.

"Hurry, children!" Mother called out above the shrieking winds. "We must get home before the snow starts falling! The clouds look like they're ready to open up at any time."

Caroline squinted up at the sky as they hurried along. Even though it was only midday and they hadn't yet eaten dinner, monstrous gray clouds filled the sky and made it look as dark as nighttime. Wishing she could feel soft wet snowflakes on her cheeks instead of the dust and dirt that scraped her skin, Caroline held her arm up in front of her face and began to wonder if the awful wind would ever go away.

Focusing on the ground in front of her, Caroline tried to remember all the stories she had heard again and again about their last Christmas with Father. The year before he went away, Father had carved little wooden dolls for his girls, and the checkerboard for the boys. Mother had cooked a meal that was so enormous, there had hardly been any room left on the table for dishes or cups. There was a goose full of fruit stuffing, turkey and ham, squash, onions, and potatoes, baked apples, plum pudding, and a mince pie for dessert. Father had declared Mother's Christmas dinner a feast fit for a king, and had chuckled and told stories until even the fire in the hearth began to sputter and fall asleep. Caroline wished she could remember that day better. She wished that Christmas could be that happy again. If Father were still here, he'd get Mother some flour for Christmas; Caroline just knew it.

The whirling wind pushed the Quiners home to their frame house in no time at all. Grandma and Martha had already taken potatoes, onions, squash, and dried beans from the root cellar and boiled them into a stew for dinner. Caroline was very hungry, and she tried her best to like this stew that Grandma called succotash. But even though it warmed every bit of her, it still didn't help Caroline forget or stop wishing for the Christmas dinner she'd been thinking about since the cold trip home from the mill.

No one spoke during dinner except Thomas, who babbled his dismay to Mother when she forbade him to scoop up potatoes from her plate with his chubby little fingers. Finally Mother broke the silence. "Goodness glory! If I don't have the most well-mannered children. This is surely the quietest dinner we've ever had. Henry-O, you haven't even asked for a second serving. Why are you all wearing such sad faces? And the day before Christmas! Imagine!"

The children looked up from their stew, but still no one spoke. Mother clapped her hands and said brightly, "We might not have fresh bread with our dinner today, but we will surely have some flour in a day or two. We have a warm house and beds to sleep in. We must not forget our many blessings, children." Standing at the head of the table, Mother scooped up Thomas, and added, "Now, let's clean up and finish our afternoon chores. As soon as supper is over tonight, we must get to bed so that we are well rested for Christmas Day!"

"Will we ever have a Christmas feast again, Mother, like we had when Father was here?" Martha asked.

"We will have the finest celebration we can, Martha," Mother said.

The day inched along, and finally it was time for bed. Mother tucked them snugly beneath their quilts, and listened as they recited their prayers.

> *"Now I lay me down to sleep,*
> *I pray the Lord my soul to keep.*
> *If I should die before I wake,*
> *I pray the Lord my soul to take.*
> *And please bless Father and keep him in*
> *heaven with You forever. Amen."*

"And please make the wind go away, and let our table be filled with a Christmas feast. Amen." Caroline prayed so softly that even Martha couldn't hear.

Caroline listened to Mother's footsteps on the stairs. Outside, the wind howled and shrieked as it flung itself around the frame house and rattled every windowpane. Gripping the top of her quilt beneath her chin, Caroline tried to concentrate on the crackling of the fire and the creaking of the rocker instead of the terrible wind.

Soon Mother's sweet singing echoed through the house, taming the wind and the clattering panes. Savoring each note, Caroline closed her eyes and tried to imagine the musty smoke from Father's pipe that used to wander up the stairs every night while Mother sang them to sleep from her rocker down below. She clutched her covers even tighter. How she missed Father, with his pipe and the big laugh that shook his whole body and made his face turn all red. Caroline missed Father's hugs most of all. She hoped it was Christmas in heaven, too, and that Father would have a feast fit for a king.

Caroline was so busy thinking about Father, that it took a moment before she realized Mother had stopped singing. She sat up in bed. Mother never stopped singing so soon after she sat in her rocker. The house was silent except for the winds that stormed outside and the rustling noises coming from the other side of the curtain. Joseph was pulling his trousers on over his flannels. "Wait here with the girls, Henry," Caroline heard him whisper before he ran down the stairs.

Now Martha was awake too. Caroline held her hand tightly, and they crept out of bed toward the top of the stairs. Henry joined them.

"What is it, Henry?" Martha asked, her whisper quivering in the cold room.

"Where's Mother?" Caroline wondered as she looked through the railing.

"I don't know," Henry whispered, "but I'm sure not going to wait to find out."

As quietly as he could, Henry inched down the first few stairs, with Martha and Caroline close behind. They crouched behind the railing, hidden by the shadows of the dark room, and watched as Mother, her shawl wrapped tightly around her shoulders, opened the kitchen door. Joseph stood behind her. The rifle that usually hung from a hook above the door was now in his hands.

The wind pulled the door open violently, and Mother stepped backward into the kitchen, shielding her candle from the wind. The fire in the hearth tossed huge dancing shadows all over the walls of the room and lit up the figure standing in the doorway. Caroline saw a tall man carrying a large bundle over one shoulder and a small one in his other gloved hand. As Mother moved closer to the door and held her candle higher, Caroline glimpsed a brown fur cap with a black stripe down the middle and yellow hair poking out of it from all sides.

With a loud thump, the tall man dropped the big bundle onto the floor. Puffs of white dust sailed up around his boots as the man said, "Evening, ma'am, boy. A happy Christmas to you." Handing Mother the small sack he carried in his other hand, he added, "I got this from Mr. Leavenworth, but I don't need it either."

Mother stood for a moment and stared speechlessly at the tall man. "Come in out of that wind," she finally said. "We don't have much, but I can surely find something to feed you."

"Thank you for your kindness," the tall man answered, "but I must be on my way to Milwaukee if I'm to see my folks for Christmas."

Turning to Joseph, Mother took the rifle from him and said, "Run and fetch the pelts from the cellar. Hurry."

As Joseph headed for the cellar, the tall man called out above the winds, "You needn't get any pelts for me, ma'am. I'm loaded with all a man can carry right now."

"But please, you must take them," Mother cried. "It's all we have to give in exchange for your kindness, and I don't like to be beholden! Not even to the best of neighbors!"

The winds quieted for a moment as the tall man touched the tip of his cap and bowed his head. "No, thank you, ma'am. Good night." Backing out the door, he pulled it closed, and all of the wind left the house with him.

Mother stood looking at the sacks of flour and brown sugar. Then she handed the rifle to Joseph, and he returned it to its place above the door. "Help me pull this sack into the corner, Joseph. Then you must go back to bed," she said.

Caroline, Martha, and Henry bounded back into their beds. By the time Caroline was back under the covers, Mother's singing was once again calming the frenzy of the wind.

Closing her eyes, Caroline sighed happily and listened once again to every note that Mother sang. In no time at all, her dreams smelled just like Mother's Christmas bread.

Christmas Bread

The first light of Christmas morning had just begun to dimly light the room as Caroline awakened. Sleepily, she rubbed her eyes and her cold nose.

The wind had stopped howling, and though she could barely see their sleeping faces in the faint light, she could hear Martha and Eliza breathing softly beside her. It was Christmas morning!

Caroline sniffed the cold air, eagerly anticipating the sweet, fresh smell of Mother's Christmas bread, but all she could smell was wood burning in the hearth below. Surely she hadn't dreamed that the man with the fur cap had visited last night? He had delivered a sack of flour for them, and Mr. Leavenworth's brown sugar, too. Caroline was sure of it.

Caroline looked over at Martha. Martha had seen the man, too. She would know if he had really visited the frame house.

"Martha?" Caroline whispered.

Martha squinted up at her sister. "What's wrong?" she asked.

"It's Christmas morning!"

"It is still dark," Martha grumbled. She closed her eyes and snuggled deeper under the quilt. "Go back to sleep."

"But the bread, Martha," Caroline insisted. "It's Christmas morning, and I don't smell Mother's special bread."

Martha kept her eyes stubbornly shut. "Mother's still asleep, Caroline. She has to be awake if she's going to bake bread, and she won't be awake until morning. Go back to sleep."

Caroline tossed and turned and tried to sleep, but she just couldn't stop thinking about the tall man and the sack of flour. It must be sitting downstairs, waiting to be baked into loaves of bread.

Caroline couldn't wait any longer to find out. She slipped out of bed and wrapped her heavy woolen shawl around her shoulders. Her long flannels and nightgown did little to keep the frosty air that blew along the floorboards from chilling her legs and freezing her bare feet. Shivering, she crept down the cold steps into the kitchen.

The embers of last night's fire smoldered beneath a layer of gray ash, and a thick oak log burned slowly in the back of the fireplace, casting a golden glow around the hearth. Caroline peered over at the corner of the room where Mother kept her supplies. In the dim light and dark shadows, she saw what looked like a tall, fat sack resting against the wall. Merrily she clapped her cold hands together. The tall man with the fur cap had visited the frame house after all!

"Caroline Lake Quiner! You'll catch your death walking on these floorboards in your bare feet! Whatever are you doing out of bed at this hour?"

Caroline spun around to find Mother standing behind her in a gray flannel nightgown. Her long black hair hung in a single thick braid, and she looked sleepy.

"I wanted to see if the flour was still there. I wanted to see if you had started making your Christmas bread."

"Why, how did you know about the flour?" Mother asked.

Caroline took a deep breath. "You stopped singing, Mother. And then Joseph went downstairs. We heard you talking to someone at the door and . . ."

Mother finished her sentence. "And so you got out of bed to see what was happening."

"Yes, ma'am," Caroline said guiltily.

"Look at me when you are speaking, Caroline," Mother said firmly.

"Yes, ma'am." Caroline looked up apprehensively. But Mother was smiling.

"It certainly was a wonderful Christmas surprise, wasn't it?"

"Oh, yes!" Caroline beamed.

"You've seen the sack of flour, Caroline—now hurry back to bed. I'll have no coughs or sneezes from you on this Christmas Day!"

Caroline knew she should go quietly back to bed, but she just couldn't help asking one more question. "But Mother," she asked, "why haven't you baked any Christmas bread?"

Mother took hold of Caroline's small hands. "Goodness glory!" she cried. "You are colder than an icicle!" She settled Caroline on a chair in front of the fire and tucked her shawl snugly around her. "Keep those toes in front of the fire. By the time I show you what's happened to the Christmas bread, you will be all warm again."

Mother walked to the corner of the hearth and reached into the dough box, a big black space carved out of the bricks near the top of the hearth. She pulled out a tin pail and looked inside. Tipping it toward Caroline, Mother showed her the oversized puff of dough that filled the inside of the pail like a big pearly cloud. "I was going to wait a few more hours to knead the dough, but it looks ready. As long as we are both awake, we may as well knead it right now," she said. "Then the dough can rise while the oven heats, and we'll be baking bread soon after breakfast! Would you like to help?"

"Oh, yes!" Caroline exclaimed.

Kneeling on the chair with her toes tucked beneath her nightgown, Caroline leaned forward and watched as Mother punched the puff down in the pail and flattened it. Then Mother carefully peeled the dough out of the pail and set it on the clean tabletop. Patting it down once more, she sprinkled it with flour. In one quick movement she pulled the top of the dough toward her, flipped it over on itself, and turned the soft lump a quarter turn. Caroline watched intently as Mother pushed the dough-ball forward, pulled it, flipped it, and turned it. Caroline tried to count the number of times Mother turned and pushed the dough, but she ran out of numbers that she knew long before Mother finished kneading.

"All right, Caroline," Mother finally said. "Would you like to try?"

"Yes, yes!" Caroline cried.

Mother dropped the dough in front of Caroline and moved behind her. Caroline pushed on the soft dough just as she had seen Mother do it. When it came time to flip and turn the dough, Mother put her hands over Caroline's, and together they finished kneading.

"Now stay here while I grease a bowl."

Mother quickly returned to the table with the greased bowl, and Caroline scooped up the doughball and gently placed it inside with one final pat. "There, now." Mother looked pleased. "We just have to wait a few hours for the dough to rise again. I'm going to set a fire on the floor of the bake oven so it will be ready for baking. Wash your hands and get back to bed now, Caroline. You can surely catch a few winks before your sisters and brothers wake up."

As Caroline headed up the stairs, she looked back to see Mother filling the floor of the little bake oven with small sticks and shavings of firewood.

"Thank you for letting me help, Mother," Caroline called from the stairs.

"You did a fine job, Caroline. Sleep well now."

Back beneath the warm quilt, Caroline closed her eyes and tried one last time to sleep. But the morning light filling the room and the excitement of Christmas kept her wide awake. It seemed like a whole day instead of just one hour before she and her sisters and brothers were rushing down the stairs for Christmas breakfast.

"Merry Christmas, children," Mother called.

"Merry Christmas!" Caroline sang as she searched the table for the bowl of bread dough. The table was already laid for breakfast, and beside every tin cup was a little bundle wrapped in a swatch of red calico and tied with a pretty loop of twine.

"Oh, Mother," Caroline said. "They're so pretty!"

"What's inside?" Martha asked eagerly.

"As soon as you finish your breakfast, you may open them and find out," Mother answered, her eyes twinkling.

Caroline was so busy staring at her little

bundle and wondering what was inside, she scarcely noticed the piles of steaming hotcakes that Grandma carried to the table. She didn't notice Mother pouring the milk or trickling molasses over each plate of hotcakes. As she absentmindedly took her first bite of hotcake, Caroline was surprised to find that the hotcakes didn't taste like cornmeal. "Oh!" she sighed with pleasure. They were rich and thick and smooth and quite possibly the best hotcakes she had ever tasted.

Soon Henry surveyed the table to make certain that every last bit of hotcake had been eaten and every last drop of milk swallowed. "May we open our bundles now, Mother?" he asked hopefully.

"If you are finished eating, Henry, then everyone else must be, too," Mother chuckled. "Go ahead, children. Open your surprises."

Caroline grabbed her bundle and tugged eagerly at the twine. Inside the calico pouch was a pair of red mittens exactly her size. Martha and Eliza also had red mittens. Joseph's and Henry's were dark blue.

"Try them on, children!" Mother urged, bouncing Thomas on her knee.

Caroline slid one of her mittens over her fingers. Her fingertips felt something smooth and round. Two things. Maybe even three.

"There's something inside!" Caroline shouted.

"In mine, too!" Martha said.

"Mine, too!" Eliza repeated with a giggle.

Pulling her mitten off, Caroline held her hand open beneath it and shook it until three round circles fell out.

"Buttons!" Caroline said delightedly.

"Look! One of mine has a house on it!" Martha held her button high above her head so everyone could see. "And I think it's china!"

"Yes, it is china, Martha." Mother laughed. "Every girl must begin her button collection with a china button."

Caroline's china button had a tree and four tiny flowers that looked like little red snowflakes painted on it. Her biggest button was a gleaming gold, and as Caroline held it up, it flashed little white dots all over the walls. The last button had red and blue stripes and was made out of soft cloth. Caroline could hardly imagine a dress pretty enough to deserve such a button.

"Oh, thank you, Mother!" Caroline called out as she lined her buttons on the table and studied them more closely.

"You each have another mitten, girls, do you not?" Mother's eyes twinkled.

Caroline reached for her other mitten. She shook it eagerly and gasped. A thin red-and-white-striped candy stick had fallen into her hand.

"Henry, look!" Caroline cried. "Candy!"

"I got one, too, little Brownbraid." Henry winked.

"May we eat it now, Mother?" Martha begged.

"You may do as you like," Mother said as she stood up. "Just remember, you have only one piece. So savor every bit of it."

The sweet, fresh taste of the peppermint tickled Caroline's mouth, and she laughed with pleasure. "It's so delicious!" she exclaimed, and then she remembered her brothers had mittens, too. "Henry, Joseph, what did you find in your mittens?" she asked curiously.

"We both got horses!" Henry held up the miniature horse he had pulled out of his mitten. It was carved out of well-worn, dark shiny wood and was trotting with its head held high. Joseph's horse stood tall and fierce on its hind legs. They were perfectly shaped and looked so real that Caroline half expected them to run across the table and out of the frame house.

"Those are very special horses, Henry," Grandma spoke up. "Your father carved them for me when he was not much older than Joseph."

"Father made them?" Joseph asked. He ran his fingertips gently across the smooth wood of his horse as though it was the most precious object he had ever held.

"Yes, Joseph," Grandma answered. "When I was very young, my father, your great-grandfather, owned many horses. I tended and rode them for years. Your father inherited my love for horses. As soon as he was old enough to carve, he began whittling away on scraps of wood, and most of his pieces eventually became horses. He carved these two horses for me one Christmas long ago. They were two of my favorites."

"Oh, Joseph, can I hold it?" Caroline burst out as Grandma finished her story.

"Me first, Caroline," Martha countered. "I'm older."

"You may play with the horses after the boys finish filling the wood box and we clear the table and wash the dishes." Mother smiled down at Grandmother as she handed Thomas to her, but it seemed to Caroline that the sparkle in her eyes had dimmed. "I must get our Christmas bread into the oven if we are ever to taste it today."

As soon as the dishes were back in the dish dresser, Mother said, "Now, Martha, help Grandma prepare her sweet potatoes and dried apples for dinner. Caroline and I must finish the job we started early this morning."

Martha watched curiously as Caroline followed Mother to the bake oven. The bowl that only a few hours earlier had cradled the flattened ball of dough now held a smooth, puffy cloud that reached to the rim.

"Is it ready to bake yet?" Caroline asked.

"The dough's ready, Caroline," Mother answered. "Let's see about the oven."

Carefully, Mother put her hand into the oven to test the temperature. "I think it's ready. Let's get the bread onto the peel."

Mother lifted the dough from the bowl and separated it into six long, thin sections. After twisting and patting the strands of dough into two long braids, Mother sprinkled the tops with a crumbly mixture of brown sugar, flour, and molasses.

"As soon as I lift the dough, Caroline, slide the peel beneath it as fast as you can."

Once the braids of bread were safely on the peel, Caroline set the flat wooden paddle on the table and looked at them. The hotcakes she'd eaten for breakfast had chased her hunger away, but just the sight of Mother's Christmas bread made her feel hungrier than ever. Dinner could not come soon enough.

Mother quickly raked out the fire in the oven, slid the braids of dough into the dough box, and sealed its opening with the heavy door.

"There!" she said as the door clicked shut. "We may not have a Christmas feast this year, girls, but we will have our Christmas bread."

"Add to that a bit of plum pudding!"

Mr. Carpenter's loud laugh filled the kitchen, and Caroline whirled around to find him standing beside the kitchen door. He was holding a large bowl, and his dark eyes were as merry as his smile.

"Up! Up! Up!" Thomas heard Mr. Carpenter's laugh, and scooted to the corner of the settle where he had been busy playing.

"Well, hello, old boy!" Mr. Carpenter called out to him.

"Goodness glory, my heart's beating faster than a jackrabbit running from a grizzly!" Mother exclaimed. "Whatever brings you here, Benjamin?"

"Why, Christmas of course, Charlotte!

Forgive me for startling you so. I followed young Henry in on one of his trips from the woodpile. You and little Miss Caroline were so busy with your fixings, I didn't have the heart to interrupt." Mr. Carpenter added, "That bread looks too delicious to eat, Caroline. I hope you'll save a piece for your old friend Mr. Ben."

"Oh, yes!" Caroline smiled up at him.

"Will you be staying?" Mother asked. "The boys will be back inside in no time, and I'm certain they would love to visit."

"As would I. But my Sarah made me promise I'd deliver this plum pudding and get back without delay. The house is filled to the rafters with hungry aunts and uncles, and seems they always discover when I sneak off." Handing the bowl of pudding to Mother, Mr. Carpenter crossed the room and pulled Thomas out of the settle. Throwing him up into the air, he called out over the baby's delighted cries, "I'll be back to visit in a day or so. Meantime, happy Christmas to you and yours, Charlotte. And don't you eat up all this pudding by yourself, young Thomas," he said, tweaking the baby's nose.

"The Lord loveth a cheerful giver, Benjamin. Thank you, and send our thanks to Sarah, also."

The sweet, fresh smell of Mother's Christmas bread was already filling the room as Mother closed the door behind Mr. Carpenter. Caroline and Martha hurried over to look inside the bowl of plum pudding.

"Run and play with your Christmas presents now, girls. It will be a while before dinner is ready."

Mother's eyes were sparkling again as Caroline and Martha took Eliza and ran off to play with their buttons and lick their sticks of candy.

As the three girls compared buttons, Caroline gazed up at Father's wooden horses that were standing proudly on the mantel above the hearth. It didn't matter that there would be no goose stuffed with fruit stuffing, fresh turkey, or ham on their table for Christmas dinner. They had Mother's Christmas bread, Grandma's sweet potatoes and baked apples. They even had some plum pudding. And candy. And mittens and buttons. And most special of all, Father's horses. It was a wonderful Christmas, after all.

Wagon Pie

Bent over a slate scribbled with numbers, Martha rested her chin in her hand and sighed heavily. Caroline, too, felt the dullness of the long winter day spreading over the frame house like a heavy gray blanket. And the hungry tightness in her stomach didn't help matters.

"When will Henry and Joseph be home, Mother?" Martha asked. Henry and Joseph had started going to school right after Christmas. Every morning they left the house after breakfast and trudged almost three miles to the schoolhouse through drifts of blowing snow. They rarely returned home before darkness fell.

"At suppertime, as they are every day," Mother answered. "Why do you ask?"

"Oh, I just hoped they might come home early today," Martha said. She raised her head and looked at Mother, her big eyes shining. "A fresh snow fell last night, and I so want to play fox and geese!"

Listening closely for Mother's answer, Caroline looked up from the yellowed paper she was studying. It was filled with Bible verses and was the very same study sheet that Mother had used when she was a girl back in Boston. Mother had given it to all of her children when they were first learning to read and spell. Caroline liked to study from this page of verses, because even if she could read only the littlest words, she still knew what every verse said. Mother made her and Martha recite them daily. Caroline had memorized the whole page.

"It's time for your lessons now, Martha, not for playing. Sit up straight and begin your sums. You can return to your readings later."

Mother looked up from her mending and saw a glum look settle on Martha's face, so she brightened her voice and added, "Perhaps if the boys come home before dusk and you've finished your lessons, you can all play outside for a short time before supper."

Caroline looked back at her page of verses and wished with all her might that Joseph and Henry would arrive home in time to play outside. Fox and geese was Caroline's favorite game to play in the snow, but she and Martha couldn't play it without Joseph and Henry, because they needed more than one goose to chase. Since the boys had started school, they hadn't been able to play it once.

Sitting up straight, Martha grumbled, "It's not fair that I have to study here when Joseph and Henry can go to the schoolhouse."

Mother raised an eyebrow. "Your brothers and all the boys in town go to school in the wintertime because they are needed at home and in the fields at other times of the year when there's so much work to be done. With so many older boys attending school in the schoolhouse, there simply isn't room for all the young ladies in Brookfield to go to school with them. You will have lessons in the schoolhouse this summer, Martha, just as you did last summer. And this summer Caroline will go to school with you. And unless you both begin studying your books, come June you'll find that you haven't kept up with the other scholars in your class. Now, stop your complaints and recite your multiplication tables."

Chastened, Martha looked down at her sums. "Three times five is fifteen," she began in a small voice.

Caroline looked down at her page of verses without really seeing the beautifully scripted words. One curving letter blended into the next as she listened to Martha and wished that she, too, could go to the schoolhouse with Joseph and Henry. After all, Henry didn't even like sitting through lessons, and just this morning he had told Mother he would gladly give up his seat for the day. Caroline thought that Mother should let her go to school instead of Henry. Martha only wanted to go to school so she could be with her brothers; she didn't want to go there to study. But Caroline loved learning to read and write, and she could not wait for summer to hurry back to Brookfield so she could go to the schoolhouse and have her very own reader, one with crisp, clean pages instead of the crumpled, stained sheets of paper in the reader that her brothers and sister had learned from first. Besides, she was sure that lessons would go much faster in a schoolhouse than they did at her own table.

Eliza and Thomas were napping soundly, and Grandma Quiner sat quietly knitting at the sewing table with Mother. The house was silent except for the sputtering of the fire and the scratching of Martha's pencil against her slate. Moving on the hard seat of her chair, Caroline tried to focus again on her Bible verses, but the grumbles in her hungry stomach made her forget the words as soon as she read them. It seemed as though their small dinner had ended hours ago, and supper would never come.

"Caroline, have you completed a new verse yet?" Mother asked.

"Yes, Mother." Caroline shifted again in her chair and looked at the paper on the table below.

"Please recite it to me."

Reading Mother's neat script slowly and carefully, Caroline sounded out the first few words, and then recited the rest of the verse, which she knew by heart. " 'It is e-easier for a c-camel to pass through the eye of a needle than for a rich man to enter the kingdom of heaven.' "

"Very good!" Mother praised.

"What is a camel?" Caroline asked.

"A very large animal that has a hump on its back and stands on four long, thin legs. It lives in a place called the desert where it is very, very hot."

"Have you ever seen a camel or a desert?"

"Only in pictures," Mother said.

Wrinkling her brow, Caroline asked, "Well, if it's such a big animal, Mother, then how could it ever fit through the eye of a tiny needle?"

"That's the lesson in the verse, Caroline. It would be nearly impossible for a camel to fit through the eye of a needle. So would it be even less possible for a rich man to enter the kingdom of heaven."

"Are we rich?" Caroline asked.

"No, Caroline," Mother answered. "We are not rich."

"Well, then, it's good that we are not rich, Mother!" Suddenly Caroline felt much better. She didn't ever want to be rich if it meant that she could never enter the kingdom of heaven. Father was in heaven, and she wanted to go and see him there someday.

"I, for one, wish we *were* rich!" Martha interrupted her sister's thoughts as she banged her slate pencil down on her slate.

"Martha!" Mother exclaimed.

"If we were rich, we could have pretty new dresses and shoes, and food to eat whenever we wanted it!" Martha looked at Mother, bit her bottom lip, and looked down again at her slate. "I'm sorry, Mother," she whispered.

"You *have* a dress and shoes, Martha, and we have perfectly fine food to eat," Mother reprimanded her. "You must never complain about what you have or don't have. We are very fortunate."

"But I'm hungry, Mother," Martha whispered. When she finally looked up at Mother, there were tears in the corners of her eyes.

"We will have supper as soon as your brothers arrive home." Mother's voice was kind but firm. "The time will pass quickly if you finish your sums."

Martha dropped her chin back into her hand and picked up her slate pencil. Caroline looked back at her verses and had just begun sounding out a new verse when the kitchen door swung open and the cold winter air blew into the house with Joseph and Henry.

"Goodness glory!" Mother exclaimed. She set down her mending and hurried across the room to shut the open door. "Whatever are you boys doing home so early in the afternoon?"

Caroline and Martha sat very still as Joseph unwrapped his scarf from around his neck and mouth and said breathlessly, "The schoolmaster sent everyone home early today, Mother."

"Shake that snow off your boots by the door,

Henry-O!" Mother said, wiping up the small puddles of water forming on the wooden planks around Henry's boots. "Now, what happened, Joseph?"

"After recess, Danny McCarthy brought a huge snowball back into the schoolhouse and left it on the schoolmaster's chair."

Caroline and Martha held their breath, waiting to hear what happened next. Joseph continued. "Mr. Henderson was none too pleased when he came back into the room and sat down right in the middle of a cold, wet pile of slush."

Henry burst into laughter that echoed all around the kitchen. "You should have seen it, Mother!" he roared. "I never saw anybody jump so high! Why, he practically hit the rafters!"

Caroline wanted to laugh too, but a quick glance at Mother's stern face kept her quiet. "How dare that Daniel McCarthy," Mother said fiercely. "He's been nothing but trouble since he and his folks arrived in Brookfield. I hope the schoolmaster punished him but good for his disrespect!"

"He tried, Mother," Joseph answered, "but Danny's friends cornered him by the door and locked him outside before he ever had a chance to strike Danny."

"Old Man Henderson was standing outside until Joseph opened the door for him again!" Henry added proudly. "Weren't for Joseph, he'd be a big old icicle by now."

"That's enough, Henry." Mother's voice was still angry. "You will call the schoolmaster Mr. Henderson."

"Yes, ma'am." Henry tried to keep a straight face but was unable to stifle his grin.

"It was good of you to help, Joseph." Mother's voice softened as she patted his shoulder.

"Danny and his friends didn't think so. As soon as Mr. Henderson came back inside, he told them that they could never return to the schoolhouse. Then he sent the rest of us home. Danny, Mike, and Frank followed Henry and me most of the way." Joseph's voice was steady, but his eyes were bright with excitement.

Caroline watched as Mother's eyes became more worried than angry. "Was there any trouble?" she asked.

"Except for a few flying snowballs, those boys couldn't touch us!" Henry said, and he slapped his hand on his knee. "We ran much too fast. And, besides, Joseph is bigger than all of 'em, and I'm almost as big as one or two!"

"You did the right thing, boys," Mother said. "Now take off your coats and warm yourselves by the fire. We'll have an early supper tonight."

"But Mother!" Martha stood up from the table and called out, "You said that if Joseph and Henry came home early, we could play outside before supper! Can't we please go out and play fox and geese?"

"Have you finished your sums, Martha?" Mother inquired.

"Almost all of them, Mother. I can finish the others tomorrow. I promise I will." Clasping her hands together, Martha pleaded, "Please, may we go outside before it is dark?"

"Oh, please?" Caroline chimed in hopefully.

"Well, it *is* a special treat to have your brothers home early." Mother relented. "Just this once, you may put off your sums until tomorrow. Wear both mittens and scarves. It's very cold outside."

As soon as they were all bundled up, Mother opened the door, and Caroline, Martha, Henry, and Joseph ran out into a yard of fresh snow that sparkled in the sunlight. The wind had all but disappeared, but the frigid air still stung the inside of Caroline's nose as she took a deep breath and ran after her brothers and sister.

"Let's make the circle fast!" Joseph shouted.

Together, they began to stamp the newly fallen snow into a gigantic circle. Joseph and Henry pushed their way through knee-deep drifts of ice and snow, while Caroline and Martha followed and stomped over their tracks until the snow was packed firmly on the ground.

As soon as the outside circle was completed, Henry and Joseph trudged through its thick, undisturbed center, neatly cutting four intersecting trails. Then they ran to the point where all the trails met and stomped out a small circle right in the center of the big circle.

"All ready!" Henry bellowed. He and Joseph stood back to admire their work, and Caroline and Martha ran down the lumpy snow trails and met them in the middle of the circle.

"I think it looks just like a wagon wheel," Joseph said.

"Reminds me of one of Mother's pies cut into eight huge, snowy pieces!" Henry countered.

"A wagon pie!" Caroline cried. "We'll call it our wagon pie!"

"Wagon pie it is." Joseph laughed. "Now, let's pick a fox."

"You be the fox, this time, Caroline," Henry said, his words turning into wisps of frosty steam.

Beneath the blue winter sky, Caroline, Martha, Joseph, and Henry formed a circle and held out their mittened fists.

Caroline clapped her mittens together and counted around the circle of hands, hitting a different fist with every word she spoke.

"Wire, briar, limber lock,
Three geese in a flock.
One flew east, one flew west,
One flew over the cuckoo's nest.
O-U-T . . . OUT!"

With that, Henry, Joseph, and Martha ran up and down and all around the trails of the wagon pie as fast as they could, trying to get back to the inner circle before Caroline caught them.

Henry arrived at the inner circle first. "Home free!" he called.

"Home free!" Martha called as she tumbled in next to Henry, huffing and laughing out little puffs of foggy breath at the same time.

"I . . . GOT YOU, Joseph! You're IT!" Caroline screamed. She lunged after her oldest brother as he ran toward the inner circle and caught the bottom corner of his jacket just before she slipped and fell into a powdery bank of snow. Arms pinwheeling in the air, Joseph danced on the slippery ground for a few seconds before he slipped and tumbled with a big *crunch!* right next to Caroline.

Laughing and running as fast as they could, Henry and Martha scampered down a trail of the wagon pie and pulled Joseph and Caroline up from their chilly nest of snow. Martha brushed chunks of snow and ice from Caroline's scarf, shawl, and braid, and took hold of her mittened hand. Together they skipped and slid back to the center circle, where Joseph now called out the fox's rhyme so loudly that it echoed across all the snow-covered trees.

Pink wisps of clouds hung from the sky as the sun dropped below the pine tree horizon and the afternoon light turned from blue to golden orange. Caroline and Martha and Henry and Joseph chased each other up and down the wagon-pie trails until the golden orange faded to a dark purple-blue, and Mother called them inside for supper.

"I for one am sure glad Danny McCarthy caused so much trouble today!" Henry burst out as they headed back to the house.

"Henry!" Joseph admonished. Then he laughed. "Me, too!"

"I wish someone would cause all that trouble *every* day!" Martha dreamed aloud. "Imagine! We could play fox and geese all day long!"

"Me, too," Caroline sang out. Her toes and fingers were tingly with cold, her cheeks frozen red, but she didn't mind at all. Shivering and happy, she crunched through the snow all the way back to the snug frame house.

Such a Treat

Caroline finished fluffing the pillows and arranged them neatly on the bed. "I'm going to get the broom, Martha," she said.

"Maybe you could bring us something to eat, too," Martha whispered as she dusted the chest.

Caroline knew that Martha was only half joking. The Quiners had eaten nothing for breakfast but small bowls of cornmeal mixed with water and a pinch of salt. "Mother's mush," Henry called it. Mother had cooked only enough for one bowl each, and though

Caroline didn't like mush at all, she was so hungry, she could have eaten two bowls of it that morning, maybe even three.

"I could ask Mother," Caroline whispered back. "I know she has a little of that sack of flour left; I heard her tell Grandma. Maybe she'd bake a small loaf of bread if we asked."

Martha shook her head. "You must not ask. Just bring the broom."

Caroline nodded and headed down the stairs. When she reached the bottom step, she saw Joseph standing at the door, his coat and hat covered with fresh snow. Fat flakes had been falling from cloudy gray skies almost every day since that afternoon they had stamped out the wagon pie. For the last three days, Joseph and Henry had been unable to cross the deep banks of snow that blocked the paths to the schoolhouse. They were home all day now, having lessons at the table with Caroline and Martha. But the snow was too high for any games of fox and geese. Caroline couldn't see the wagon pie anymore, nor could she see the logs in the woodpile or the huge twisted roots that dipped up and down and crisscrossed the frozen ground beneath the trunk of the mighty oak. Everything in sight was covered with a heavy blanket of white, and the falling snow had no intention of stopping.

"We didn't find anything," Caroline overheard Joseph telling Mother. "Every trap was empty."

"I don't suppose there's any chance of catching fish today?" Mother asked. Peering out the window, she murmured to herself, "Of course there isn't. So much snow has fallen in the last week and a half, it would take a whole day just to clear a path to the ice on the river. Never mind trying to cut a fishing hole through it."

Caroline saw the worry on Mother's face as she looked back at Joseph, and she decided not to interrupt them. Her sweeping could wait. But the stairs creaked beneath her feet as she headed upstairs, and she turned back to find Mother and Joseph now looking up at her from the kitchen.

"Have you and Martha finished tidying your room?" Mother asked.

"I came to get the broom," Caroline answered.

Mother beckoned her back downstairs. "It's over by the hearth."

Caroline stepped into the kitchen as Mother continued speaking to Joseph. "We'll just have to use what's left in the root cellar, Joseph. We've gone without meat for longer than this." Mother's voice was now more cheerful, though her face was still troubled.

"I'm going to help Henry clear the snow from the woodpile," Joseph said. Pulling the flaps of his coat tightly together beneath his chin, he opened the door. Brilliant sunshine and a blast of cold air rushed into the kitchen. "We'll be back soon with fresh wood, Mother. We'll need to leave it in front of the fire so it can dry out some before we put it in the wood box with the rest of the logs."

Mother closed the door tightly behind Joseph and turned back to Caroline. "I was just about to sweep when your brother came in," she said. "I'll go gather the turnips in the cellar while you sweep your room, Caroline, and I'll finish up here as soon as you bring the broom back."

Turnips for supper again! Caroline was suddenly not very hungry anymore. She longed to protest, but instead she said as cheerfully as she could, "I'll hurry with the broom, Mother."

Three loud thumps *bang, bang, bang*ed at the kitchen door, stopping Caroline in her tracks. Heart pounding, she turned and ran behind Mother.

"Gracious!" Mother exclaimed. She let go of the heavy cellar door, and it slammed shut as she hurried to the kitchen door. "How could Joseph and Henry have cleared all that snow from the woodpile so quickly? And why are they pounding on the door like that?"

Caroline peeked out from behind Mother's scratchy wool skirt as Mother pulled the kitchen door open. Sunlight rushed back into the room, and the outlines of two figures slowly came into focus as Caroline's eyes adjusted to the brilliant glare. Joseph stepped in front of one sunbeam, and Caroline saw a large hand on his shoulder.

Mother moved swiftly toward Joseph. "What's wrong?" she asked. "What's happened?"

Joseph's mouth opened as though he was about to speak, but instead of Joseph's voice, Caroline heard a very different voice: a deep and hurried voice speaking in words she could not understand.

Startled, Mother stepped back into the kitchen, her face white. Caroline's breath caught in her throat as a man stepped into the room in front of Joseph. The strange voice belonged to an Indian.

Thick black hair framed the Indian's face and fell down around the shoulders of his tan leather coat. His eyes were black and sparkling, and a jagged scar stretched from the corner of his left eye all the way down his red-brown cheek to the side of his chin. He spoke excitedly, his long black hair flipping from one side of his face to the other as he nodded and gestured to Mother.

In a strained and almost unrecognizable voice Mother demanded, "What is it you want?"

Joseph now pushed his way into the room beside the Indian. His light brown hair was tousled, and his cheeks were bright red from the cold. "Don't be afraid, Mother," Joseph said. "This man is Crooked Bone. You met him once with Father. When Father took us hunting, Crooked Bone often found us in the woods and showed us how to set traps and kill game quickly. Father told us that he and his people lived here long before us or any of our neighbors. Now Crooked Bone only comes back to hunt and fish."

Mother did not move, but Caroline could feel her relaxing a little. "I do remember him now. What does he want, Joseph? Does he know that Father is not here?"

"He's brought us meat, Mother!" Joseph cried joyfully. "More meat than even Henry could eat!"

"Meat!" echoed Crooked Bone. "Bring here!" Pointing to the floor beneath his snowy boots, Crooked Bone shouted to someone outside.

"Wait! Wait!"

Caroline couldn't see Henry beyond the door, but she heard his plea, and her stomach flipped again.

Mother started toward the door and then stopped immediately. She stepped back slowly as a second Indian entered the room. He too had long black hair that hung straight down around his face and shoulders. Deep wrinkles lined his face, and his forehead was damp with sweat. He stared intently at the floor, pulling with all his might on a taut, gnarled rope that stretched past his shoulder out the door. Huffing and puffing, he struggled forward.

"Don't bring that in there! Wait!"

Again Caroline heard Henry yelling outside, but the Indian didn't seem to hear or understand. He just kept pulling on the rope, and soon two long branching horns slid into the room. Suddenly, the front half of a large buck was lying in the doorway of the kitchen, frosty white patches of snow and ice caked on its chestnut-brown fur.

Henry poked his head in through the door. "Sorry, Mother," he said. "I tried to stop them from bringing it in the house."

Mother scarcely noticed that Henry was speaking. Her eyes wide and unbelieving, she looked from the buck to the Indians and exclaimed, "This is for us? The whole animal?"

Wiping the sweat from his brow, the Indian with all the wrinkles looked down at the buck and remained silent. Crooked Bone clapped his hands together and smiled. Pointing at Henry and Joseph, he said, "See boy in forest." He held his open palms together. "Trap empty many sun, many moon." Shaking his fists, Crooked Bone added, "Boy of Red-Hand hungry. Red-Hand friend."

"Red-Hand?" Mother looked away from the Indian and turned to Henry and Joseph. "Who he is talking about?"

"Father," Joseph answered.

Mother nodded and murmured, "Father's scar from making the candlesticks."

Crooked Bone stepped back in the doorway and Caroline held her breath as he leaned over the buck and pulled an arrow from its shoulder. "Meat," he said. "Red-Hand boy eat."

Mother looked from the buck to Crooked Bone. "Thank you," she said. "Thank you."

Crooked Bone nodded and said, "Red-Hand friend." Then he reached down and pulled a thick silver blade from his leather pants. He knelt before the head of the buck and raised the gleaming knife.

Caroline hid her face in her hands as Mother cried, "Wait! Stop! Joseph, Henry-O," Mother ordered, "help these men pull the deer into the barn. You can help them skin and cut it there, and you can bring me the meat. We'll roast the haunch tonight and smoke the loins so they won't spoil."

Caroline began to shiver. Bitter-cold winter air had been blowing in through the door ever since the Indians had entered the house. Henry and Joseph pointed at the barn, and then they helped the men drag the buck out of the doorway. Mother shut the door behind them and turned to Caroline. "We have a lot of work to do if we're to eat any of this meat for supper, Caroline," she said briskly. "Go call Martha. I'll get Grandma from the parlor."

Caroline ran up the stairs so fast that she was almost out of breath when she reached the top. "We have meat, Martha!" Caroline cried. "The Indians came, Father's friends! They brought us meat. A whole deer! Come downstairs now. We have to help Mother."

"Eliza help, too!" Eliza pleaded.

Martha turned to Caroline, her eyes wide with wonder. "We heard all the commotion, and I didn't think I should bring Eliza downstairs. Oh, Caroline, I missed it! Are they still here?"

"They're going to the barn with Henry and Joseph. But maybe you can still see them out the window if you hurry," Caroline said.

Martha clattered down the stairs with Eliza in her arms and Caroline right behind her. Caroline's head spun thinking about the Indians and their wonderful gift, and she felt hungrier than ever. Why, she would even happily eat turnips again, if she could eat them with meat!

Mother stood in front of the fire, poking the logs with a black iron stick. Orange and gold sparks popped out of the wood from all sides and soared up the chimney. "Move the broom away from the hearth, Caroline," Mother said. "We need a brisk fire to cook all that meat, and I don't want anything near the hearth that might catch fire."

Henry burst through the door as Caroline was moving the broom. "Here it is!" he shouted, and he lugged the first slab of fresh venison to the hearth.

Mother looked closely at the meat. "It's so lean," she said. "The deer must be having trouble finding food in all this snow, too. If only we had some butter or bacon fat to baste it." Tapping her finger against her chin, she sighed. "It matters not. Let's get it roasting."

As soon as Mother finished hanging the venison over the fire, she placed a shallow pan directly beneath it. Caroline watched closely as Mother stood before the hearth, carefully turning the meat. "Such a treat!" she exclaimed. "We must be sure to cook it evenly!"

After turning the meat, Mother stoked the logs, setting off a whole new flurry of sparks.

Caroline held her breath as a few of the sparks flew onto Mother's heavy wool skirt. Mother dropped the poker, quickly beat out the sparks, and then turned back to the meat.

Tiny drops of juice began to drip into the basting pan as the meat slowly cooked. "There is some fat, after all," Mother marveled. She carefully pulled the basting pan from the fire with a long pair of iron tongs and poured the drippings back over the meat. "Such a treat!" She smiled. "We musn't let it get too dry!"

Soon Henry and Joseph and the two Indians were back at the house with the rest of the venison, much of it now cut into thin strips. Crooked Bone walked over to Mother, and showed her the strips he held in his hand. "Pemmican!" he said. "Keep long time."

Caroline had never heard of anything called pemmican before, and neither had Mother.

"Cook it on the fire?" she asked Crooked Bone.

"Cook slow," said Crooked Bone. "Dry and keep long time."

Crooked Bone began hanging long pieces of twine from the wooden mantel above the hearth. The other Indian tied strips of meat to the twine. The front of the hearth was soon covered with chunks and strips of meat that slowly roasted and dried.

"So much meat!" Mother stood back and admired all their hard work. "We'll have enough until spring, if we use it sparingly. Henry, Joseph, stay here and turn the meat while I boil some water. Martha, bring me an onion from the cellar. Caroline, put a tiny bit of flour into a small bowl and bring it to me. We must make these drippings into gravy." Wiping her brow, she added happily, "Gravy! Such a treat!"

Mother turned to Crooked Bone and his friend. "You will stay for supper?"

"Crooked Bone go . . . Red-Hand boy eat."

"Thank you for your kindness." Mother smiled at Crooked Bone, her eyes sparkling with tears that never fell.

"Red-Hand friend," Crooked Bone said solemnly. Then he and his companion went through the door and were gone.

Darkness fell long before supper was ready that night. The meat strips hung before the jumping, crackling flames in the hearth, cooking slowly. The warm house was filled with the sweet musky smell of freshly roasted venison, and the table was laden with meat, corn bread, turnips, and gravy as the Quiners finally gathered for supper. Together, they prayed.

> *"Be present at our table, Lord;*
> *Be here and everywhere adored.*
> *These mercies bless, and grant that we*
> *May feast in paradise with thee."*

Mother added, "For this special blessing we are ever thankful, Lord." And for the first time Caroline could ever remember, Mother didn't say one word when Henry asked for another piece of meat.

Cakes and Candlesticks

Caroline tapped her feet restlessly on the floor beneath her chair. Laying her sampler on the sewing table, she crossed over to the window and peered outside at the gloomy day. Dark clouds had chased all the blue from the sky. Raindrops pelted the windowpanes and slipped lazily to the bottom of the glass.

Earlier that morning, Mother had insisted that Joseph and Henry brave the rain and go to school. The sky was now as dark as twilight, and it wasn't even dinnertime yet. Caroline knew it would be ages before her brothers came home.

Caroline lightly traced the crooked paths of the raindrops with her fingertips. She pressed her nose up against the windowpane and looked hopefully for any sign that the sky would brighten or the rain would stop, but cold air simply seeped in around the edges of the window and chilled her face.

"Do you think that spring will ever come, Grandma?" she asked, her breath making little patches of fog on the cold glass.

"Of course it will, child," Grandma answered. "Why, it's just now April. Spring is already here."

Martha looked up from her knitting. "But if spring's here, Grandma," she said, "where is the sunshine? And where are all the flowers? And when is it ever going to stop raining and be warm enough for us to go outside? I'm so tired of being inside all the time. I want to go outside!"

"Patience, Martha," Grandma replied. "You will be outside again in no time."

No time seemed like it might take forever to come. Caroline couldn't wait for the last of the

snow to finally melt and for the world outside the window to be green instead of gray.

"What's all this I hear about spring?"

Caroline turned away from the window and looked closely at Mother as she entered the room. Caroline wondered where she had been and why her eyes looked so red. Every morning after chores, Mother was busy working at the sewing table. But this morning when Caroline and Martha came downstairs after straightening their room, Mother hadn't been at the table. She hadn't even been in the room.

"The girls were just saying how much they'd like to be outside, Charlotte," Grandma answered. "And I can't blame them. I'm eager for spring to bring warmer weather myself."

"Mother, look!" Eliza held up a small piece of white linen in one hand and a threaded needle in the other. "Stitches!"

Mother leaned over the sewing table and examined Eliza's four little stitches. "How lovely, Eliza!" she exclaimed. "Be very careful holding your needle."

"I'm watching, Charlotte."

"Thank you, Mother Quiner." Mother looked over at Caroline. "Why aren't you working on your sampler, Caroline?" she asked.

"I've almost finished stitching the *Q*," Caroline replied. "I just wanted to see if the rain had stopped."

Mother stood beside Caroline and looked out at all the dreariness. "It does seem as though it's been either snowing or raining forever," she said. "And we haven't had a celebration since Crooked Bone brought us the venison. I think we need a celebration!"

"A celebration!" Martha dropped her knitting and clapped. "What will we celebrate, Mother?"

Caroline hurried to the sewing table with Mother. "Well, it's too late to celebrate Joseph's birthday, and too early to celebrate Eliza's."

Caroline bounced into the chair beside Martha. "So what will we celebrate, then?" she urged Mother to tell.

Mother's eyes were suddenly as bright as her voice. "We'll celebrate springtime. We'll welcome the spring."

"Welcome spring!" Eliza repeated.

Mother was now surrounded by her three girls. "How will we celebrate, Mother?" Martha asked.

"Well, we have a fine dinner stewing already. The vegetables are scarce now, but at least we have a bit of this tasty meat," she said cheerfully. "Still, a fine dinner isn't enough for such an occasion. We must make a treat for our celebration, girls. Something simple but special."

Mother lifted Eliza into her arms and looked down at Martha's and Caroline's expectant faces. "Come along. Let's see what we can find in the pantry."

In no time at all, Mother had placed two eggs, a spoonful of salt, and a small bowl of flour on the table. "We can make some delightful cakes with this," she decided. "Martha, while I get the grease melting, please crack the eggs in here and beat them until they are light and fluffy." Handing a big bowl to Martha, Mother crossed to the stove while Caroline and Eliza watched Martha beat the eggs.

Mother picked up a tub full of lard, scooped a few thick spoonfuls into a deep pan, and placed it on the stove in front of the simmering pot of stew. While she waited for it to melt and heat, Mother went back to the table to check on Martha's egg mixture.

"They look perfectly fluffy, Martha." Mother nodded her approval. "We should add some salt," she said, and she sprinkled the top of the beaten eggs with a pinch of salt. With a brisk clap, Mother rubbed her hands together, shaking the last bit of salt from her fingertips over the eggs. She beat the egg mixture for another minute, and then reached for the bowl of flour.

Scooping up a small amount in a ladle, Mother handed the flour to Caroline and said, "It's your turn, Caroline. While I stir, please sprinkle this slowly over the batter."

Caroline held the ladle as carefully as she could so that none of the flour would spill over the sides. Slowly, she dusted the top of the eggs with the flour while Mother kept mixing, adding more flour until the batter was too stiff to beat.

"Thank you, Caroline," Mother said. "That will be plenty."

Once all the flour was mixed in, Mother pushed the dough together until it formed a round ball and kneaded it quickly. She then tossed a sprinkling of flour over the top of the table, pinched little pieces from the big ball of dough, and handed one each to Caroline, Martha, and Eliza.

Picking up a bit of dough and showing them how, Mother said, "Roll the piece of dough between your palms like this until it forms a little ball. Then set the ball on the table."

Each girl did as she was told, and Mother flattened their dough balls until they were just thin enough not to tear when she slowly peeled each one up from the table.

"Time to check the fat," she said as she finished rolling out a few extra dough balls for the boys and Grandma. The hot lard was sputter-

ing and popping as Mother peered into the
pan. It was time to fry the cakes. She dropped
the flattened balls in one by one as Caroline
and Martha stood on tiptoe looking into the
pan but keeping a respectful distance from the
bubbling fat.

Each little cake was immediately surrounded by tiny bubbles as it fell into the pool
of hot fat. The cakes sizzled and fried and
swelled into big doughy puffs that floated to
the surface of the pan. Within a minute or two,
every cake had flipped over in the hot fat and
turned a golden brown.

"They look so lovely, Mother!" Martha
exclaimed.

"What do you call them?" Caroline asked.

"Why, I don't rightly know, Caroline,"
Mother admitted.

"Puffcakes!" Martha guessed excitedly.

"Golden puffballs!" Caroline countered.

"Perhaps we should taste them first, and
then decide exactly what to call them," Mother
suggested. Caroline and Martha nodded, and

Mother smiled. "Now, girls, you'll have to stand back for a moment while I take the cakes out of the pan," she said. "We'll set them down to cool while we eat dinner, and they'll still be warm and crunchy when it comes time for dessert."

"But Mother," Caroline worried, "how can we eat the cakes before Henry and Joseph come home?"

"We'll save each of them a cake, Caroline." Mother smiled. "They just won't get to eat them when they're warm, like we will! Now hurry and set the table for dinner. We can't waste any time, or these cakes will get too cool and taste much less delicious!"

Caroline and Martha hurried to gather plates and cups from the dish dresser. Mother carefully lifted each cake out of the hot lard with a long-handled spoon, then set it on a flat tin that was covered with a clean rag. As she turned away from the stove and walked to the table to set the tin of cakes down, Eliza called out, "I want to see, too!"

Mother whirled around just as Eliza reached up to grab the handle of the pan on the stove. The tin banged down on the table as Mother dropped the cakes. "No!" Mother screamed, and ran toward Eliza. "Stop, Eliza!"

Grandma dropped her needlework and rushed toward the stove when she heard Mother scream. Caroline and Martha nearly dropped all the dishes they were carrying to the table. Eliza stopped her hand in midair. Her eyes filled with tears and her lip began to quiver. "I'm . . . I'm sorry," she cried as Mother gathered her up and carried her away from the hot stove.

"My little Eliza," Mother admonished as she pulled her close and stroked her soft blond curls. "You must never, never go near the stove again. Never!"

"But I didn't get to see," Eliza hiccupped between sobs.

Setting Eliza back down on the floor, Mother held her arms firmly and looked into her teary blue eyes. "Goodness sakes, Eliza, you scared the daylights out of me! I was certain you'd burn yourself worse than your father did years ago! You must never get so close to the fryer or the stove again," Mother warned, and hugged her once more. "Now go sit with Grandma while I help your sisters get dinner on the table."

Caroline looked at Martha, and she could tell from the surprise in her big sister's eyes that she was just as shocked that Mother had mentioned Father. Mother rarely spoke about Father, and when she did it was only to answer one of the children's questions.

After setting the plates on the table, Martha asked Mother hesitantly, "Would you tell us the story of the candlesticks?"

"Please, Mother," added Caroline. "We haven't heard that story since Father went away."

Mother kept her back to them and silently stirred the pemmican stew for such a long time that Caroline thought she hadn't heard their request. Then she turned around. Despite her smile, she couldn't hide the sadness in her eyes as she said, "Let's all sit down to dinner now. I will tell you the candlestick story."

After every bowl had been filled with the steaming stew, corn bread had been passed around the table, and grace had been said, Mother began her story.

"Father and I decided to be married in the middle of March. We sent notice to my folks in Boston and asked that they come to New Haven for the wedding. After weeks of waiting for a reply, we learned that none of my relatives would be able to come, and your father and I agreed that we should be married without delay. But Father needed a few more days to complete a gift he was making for me."

"Father was a silversmith then, wasn't he?" Martha asked.

"Yes, Martha. He worked in a large shop with two other silversmiths. I visited the shop when I was staying in New Haven with my uncle. It was there that I first met your father. There was a huge brick furnace in the center of the

215

shop, and Father was just placing the crucible inside it when my uncle and I walked in."

"What's a cru-sa-ble, Mother?" Caroline spoke the big word slowly.

"It's a big heavy pot that can melt silver without melting itself."

Caroline nodded, so Mother continued. "Father heated the silver until it melted. He'd then transfer it from the furnace to a big block of steel, where he pounded it into a teapot, a porringer, or a serving piece. Sometimes the silver wasn't yet hot enough to shape, so Father had to carry it back to the furnace and heat it more."

Mother paused, took another bite of stew, and chewed slowly. Perched on the edge of her seat, Caroline waited eagerly for her to continue.

"Father's job was very dangerous, but he thought nothing of the dangers. Before I ever met him, he had already broken two fingers while pounding the heavy metal with his steel hammer, so I expected a few mishaps now and then. What I feared most was that he'd be badly burned by the hot silver."

"Did you tell him so?" Caroline asked.

"I certainly did, Caroline. Father would laugh and say, 'Wouldn't be any fun if'n I were to worry 'bout such things, Charlotte! I'm careful as I need be, and 'til I have reason, I'll not borrow trouble by thinking such things!' "

"Tell us about the candlesticks, Mother!" Martha prompted.

"If I keep telling stories, I'll never get a warm bite of stew," Mother teased. "Well, our wedding day dawned a bright, cold day in late March. I was at the Reverend's early, and I waited and waited for Father to arrive for the wedding, but he never did. Here I'd left home, family, dress shop, and all for Henry Quiner, and he hadn't even bothered to come to the Reverend Cushman's and take our vows."

"What did you do?" Martha and Caroline called out together.

"I told the Reverend that I needed to wait right there in his parlor. I was certain that your father would come. The Reverend agreed, and there I sat, waiting for Father. It was long after dark when we both finally agreed that Father would probably not come."

"Oh, Mother!" Caroline cried. "Where was Father?"

"I didn't know, Caroline. I told the Reverend I would never speak to Henry again. But then the Reverend said, 'What if Henry has missed your wedding day for a very good reason?' "

Mother's eyes flashed as she repeated the Reverend's words. "I told the Reverend, 'If Henry could have been here, he would have arrived at your home long before I did. I can only believe that the Lord kept him from me today. I pray that his fate was not too terrible.' "

"This is the part when Father comes back!" Caroline clapped her hands.

Her smile now joyful, Mother finished the story. "That very moment, I opened the door to leave. There was your father, wearing a fine black jacket and a starched white shirt. His hair and beard were combed more neatly than

I had ever seen. He didn't smile at me; he didn't beg my forgiveness. He simply said, 'Unwrap your gift this minute, Charlotte, so we can have the Reverend marry us before the sunrise ends our wedding day.' "

"What did you do?" Caroline begged Mother to finish the story.

"I looked right at your father and I said, 'I will open a wedding gift only after there's been a proper wedding, Henry Quiner.' Father reached for my hand, and it was then that I discovered the bandages that covered his fingers, hand, and arm. 'Goodness glory, Henry!' I cried. 'Whatever happened to you?' Father took my arm in his and said, 'Hush, now, Charlotte. We'll have a whole lifetime for me to tell the story.' "

Tears were shining in Mother's eyes. "The Reverend married us that very moment."

"And the candlesticks?" Martha asked softly.

"They were the last silver pieces that Father ever made. The morning of our wedding day he was finishing them, and he accidentally spilled some of the hot metal on his hand and arm. Father was so badly burned that it took the doctor hours to apply salve and bandages. The burns took months to heal, and as you remember, his hand remained badly scarred. Father decided he'd give trading a try." Mother blinked the tears away as she finished her story. "I've treasured those candlesticks for fifteen years now, girls." Mother smiled. "I shall treasure them until the day I die."

"Why, Charlotte," Grandma exclaimed, "today's your anniversary!"

"Yes, Mother Quiner," Mother said softly.

"We must have the candlesticks on the table while we eat our cakes," Grandma said. "This is a celebration day, after all."

"Oh please, Mother, please!" Caroline and Martha echoed.

Mother went to get the candlesticks, and by the time she returned, Grandma, Caroline, and Martha had cleared the dinner dishes. Only the tray of cakes was left on the table. Mother set the candlesticks down on either side.

"Oh, Mother," Caroline whispered, "they're so beautiful."

Each candlestick was a long, thin silver pillar. The top of the candlestick was flattened and slightly wider than the pillar, which descended to the table in flat, wide steps. Around each pillar, Father had fashioned a delicate floral design.

Mother lovingly pressed a candle into each candlestick. Then she lit the end of a bit of tinder from a flame in the hearth and set the candles aglow.

"Now we have a real celebration." Mother looked from her candlesticks to her daughters.

In the soft glow of candlelight, she served the cakes all around the table. They were still warm and crunchy, though a few had crumbled when Mother had dropped them on the table and rushed to stop Eliza. Caroline bit into hers, and she thought that it tasted very much like a bubble might taste: light and airy and quick to disappear. Silently, she savored every bite.

It wasn't until later that night when she closed her eyes and waited for sleep that Caroline realized she had never asked Mother where she had been that morning. And they had never named the cakes. But none of that mattered now. As delicious as the cakes were, they weren't nearly as special as Mother's candlesticks. Caroline could still see them glowing brightly on the table long after she fell sound asleep.

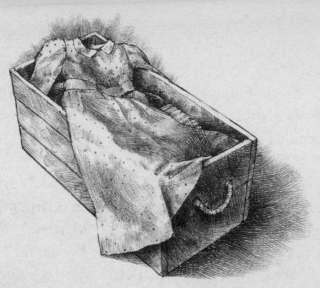

Church Dresses

The last hard chunks of grainy snow and glistening ice that clung to the tree branches and rooftops in Brookfield finally melted and drip-dropped heavily down to the ground. The sun grew warmer each day, and the bare earth gradually turned pale green. Tender blades of grass poked up from the cool dark soil, and silky, fragile leaves and buds crept out of the black, bony limbs of every maple and oak.

Caroline and Martha had just finished drying the supper dishes when they heard a loud knock at the kitchen door.

"Shall I open the door, Mother?" Martha looked over at the table where Mother was feeding Thomas.

"Please," Mother replied.

As Martha opened the door, the wide grin and sparkling dark eyes of Ben Carpenter greeted her. "Evenin', Miss Martha," He tipped his hat and smiled. "May I come in?"

"Why, of course, Mr. Ben!" Martha smiled back.

"Mr. Carpenter." Mother looked sideways at Martha.

Mr. Carpenter walked right over to the table. "Greetings, Charlotte!" he said.

Thomas immediately tried to wiggle out of Mother's arms and slide down to the floor so he could toddle over to the tall, friendly man.

"Thomas, behave yourself," Mother admonished, trying unsuccessfully to hold him.

"Come here, old boy." Mr. Carpenter grabbed Thomas and lifted him high up into the air. "Sakes alive! You're even heavier than a barrel full of nails!" He smiled down at Caroline. "And how are you, little Brownbraid?"

"Fine, thank you, Mr. Ben," Caroline replied as she stood up to greet him.

"Good golly, I think you must have grown a whole foot since last week!"

"Yes, sir," Caroline said, covering her mouth to hide her giggles. She hadn't grown a whole foot, but the bottom of her dress was falling just below her knees, and her shoes had begun to pinch her toes. She hoped Mr. Carpenter wouldn't notice how short her dress was.

Mother stood up and smoothed her apron over the front of her gray skirt. "Good evening, Benjamin. How is Sarah?"

"Sarah's a mite happier now that spring's finally here." He tossed Eliza's golden curls. "Where are the boys?"

"They're out gathering sticks to repair the fence. Is something wrong?" Mother asked.

"Not a thing, Charlotte, thank the Lord. I came by to tell you that I'm planning to yoke up the oxen bright and early Sunday morning, so Sarah, Charlie, and I can ride over to church. We thought maybe you and the children might like to come along."

"Why, thank you, Benjamin, we'd love to!" Mother's smile made her whole face shine. "I haven't brought the children to church as yet this year. I fear the ground is still too cold so early in the spring, and their shoes are nearly worn out. But if we go in the wagon, I won't have to worry about cold, wet feet!"

"We'll pass by just after breakfast, then," Mr. Carpenter said on the way to the door. "A fine night to you, ladies," he added, and pulled the kitchen door tightly closed behind him.

"Goodness!" Mother clapped her hands and turned to Caroline and Martha. "We only have two days until Sunday. You must try on your church dresses so I'll know where I have to alter them."

While Grandma watched Thomas, Mother and the girls scrambled up the stairs. Mother pulled their church dresses out of the chest and set them down on the bed. She picked up Eliza and pulled a faded red dress over her head. "This dress was too big for you last year, little Eliza," she said as she knelt in front of her and fluffed her curls. "But now it fits perfectly! And you'd never know it had been worn by your sisters before you, it's still so clean and pretty. A saving grace!"

Mother turned to Caroline. "You're next." Caroline's dress was made of soft brown cotton, with little red flowers covering it from top to bottom. She held her arms up high as Mother tried to pull her dress down over her shoulders, but it was much too tight. She even tried pulling Caroline's dress on one arm at a time and then over her head, with no luck. The dress did not fit. "My goodness, Caroline"— Mother's eyes were full of surprise—"you may have grown a whole foot, indeed!"

Martha was having the same problem. No matter how hard she tried to wiggle into it, her dress would not fit.

Mother stood up and began rubbing her chin as she puzzled over the situation. "Put your nightgown on, Martha, and hand me your dress."

Martha did as she was told, and Mother slipped Martha's church dress onto Caroline. The hem of the dress rested on the wooden plank floor, and the sleeves fell beyond Caroline's fingertips.

Looking at the dress with a critical eye, Mother pulled at the material and said to herself, "If I take it in here, and shorten it there . . . The sleeves will have to come up a bit, too . . ." She took Caroline's hands in her own and squeezed. "I think this will be just fine for you, Caroline!" she said happily. Mother then turned to Martha, who was sitting on the bed in her nightgown. "Now, as for you, Martha, downstairs I have a blue dress that I've hardly ever worn, and if I cut it down and restitch it, it will make a lovely church dress for you. Come down to the sewing table so I can measure you. Caroline, Eliza, put on your nightgowns, and Caroline, please bring your dress downstairs."

"Yes, ma'am," Caroline said as Mother and Martha headed for the stairs. Caroline looked down at Martha's old church dress, at the worn yellow cotton and the faded blue dots. Light-brown stains marked the collar, and there was a tiny hole in one sleeve. She bit her lip and tried as hard as she could to keep her tears from falling, but one big drop slipped from the corner of her eye and landed right on the dress's stained collar. "Oh, why does Martha get all the new clothes?" she said angrily as she pulled the yellow dress up over her head. "Why do *I* have to wear her old stained dresses while *she* gets to wear a brand-new one?"

"Don't be mad," Eliza whispered. Caroline tried to smile at Eliza, but she just couldn't. Two bigger drops slid down her cheeks as she helped Eliza into her nightgown and then pulled her own nightgown on over her head without ever looking up.

By the time they were standing beside the sewing table downstairs, Caroline had wiped away all her tears. Pale-blue material floated over the table as softly as a cloud floated across the sky. Caroline watched as Mother carefully measured its length and studied the seams and hem. She was humming, her forehead wrinkled, her mind busy and focused.

"Here is my dress, Mother," Caroline said.

"Thank you, Caroline," Mother said absentmindedly. "I'll begin working on your dress as soon as I finish Martha's."

When Mother wasn't watching too closely, Caroline rubbed the fabric of the blue dress gingerly between her fingers. It was soft and rich, the color so blue. There wasn't a hole or a stain on it anywhere. Caroline couldn't imagine ever wearing anything so soft and beautiful, and she knew it wouldn't stay beautiful if Martha wore it first. Next year this blue dress would be Caroline's church dress, but it would be stained and worn and tattered. She wished that she were older and bigger than Martha. Then Mother would be sewing the blue dress for her.

"Please don't touch my dress, Caroline," Martha said. "It's a perfect dress; don't get it dirty."

Caroline's cheeks felt hot as she snatched her hand away, clenched her fists, and stared back at Martha. "If I had such a perfect dress, Martha, I'd never let it get stained or dirty!" she snapped. "Not like you!"

"Enough!" Mother exclaimed as she turned

and looked straight at Caroline and Martha. "If a house be divided against itself, that house cannot stand. I will not have you speak to each other like that again." Her eyes very stern, Mother took a deep breath, and said, "Caroline, your church dress will look fine when I finish mending and shaping it. Be grateful that you have a church dress that fits you at all. And Martha, you will take extra good care of this dress so that when Caroline wears it, it will be almost as good as new. Now wash up and get to bed. Both of you."

As she splashed water over her face and rinsed soap from her hands, Caroline choked back tears. She had never made Mother so angry. She had never been so angry at Martha. Neither she nor Martha said a word to each other as they climbed the stairs and said their prayers. Caroline lay awake a long time, moving as close to the edge of the mattress as she could without falling off the bed.

Mother was busy sewing, cutting, and hemming the church dresses all the next day and evening. Caroline and Martha tried on their dresses for Mother and waited while she tucked, measured, and hemmed. Every time Mother slipped the blue dress over Martha's head, Caroline watched out of the corner of her eye. Martha's glowing face was almost as beautiful as her new blue dress. Caroline found herself wishing that Mother would forget to hem the dress, or maybe sew some old, worn buttons on it. Then she decided she just wouldn't look at the dress again. Slowly Caroline's anger turned to great disappointment, and she tried hard to pay attention to her chores and her stitches. But no matter how busy she was doing chores, eating supper, or taking a bath, her eyes kept wandering back to the sewing table and the lovely blue dress.

Sunday morning finally arrived. Mother awakened everyone well before sunup. As soon as Caroline and Martha finished their breakfast and chores, they washed their faces and hands and brushed their hair. Then Mother brought them their church dresses. Her face was flushed, her eyes bright as she helped Caroline dress first. The cotton felt soft and cool as it fell over Caroline's shoulders. The yellow dress now fit her perfectly. The sleeves hugged her wrists, and the hem was just above her ankles. Glancing down at the collar, Caroline could hardly see the stains that, only yesterday, were so dark and blotchy. Even the tiny hole had been so expertly repaired that Caroline could hardly find it.

"Thank you for making my dress so pretty, Mother," Caroline said. She smiled up at Mother and tried not to think one awful thought.

Smoothing Caroline's collar, Mother patted her shoulder. "I scrubbed extra hard to get rid of the stains, Caroline. The dress looks much brighter now, and you look very pretty in it."

Caroline flushed with pleasure as Mother helped Martha into the blue dress. "You look very pretty, too, Martha," Mother said as she finished tying the bow in the middle of Martha's back.

Caroline did not want to look at Martha in her new dress, but she just couldn't help it. The blue material looked even prettier today. The dress flowed down Martha's tall frame and seemed to float in the air just above her bare feet. Even the dresses that Mother made for Mrs. Stoddard could not compare to it.

Mother gazed critically at Martha's hem. "It might be a little bit too long, Martha, but we don't have time to shorten it before church," she said. "We'll take it up after we get home. Until then, your shoes will give you just enough height so that you won't step on the fabric." Mother looked proudly at Martha and Caroline for a moment before she added, "Put your shoes on, girls. We have very little time before the Carpenters arrive."

Caroline, Martha, and Eliza had their shoes lined up next to each other beside the chest. Caroline's and Martha's shoes looked very different. As old and scuffed as Caroline's shoes were, their worn, dark leather covered the whole of each foot. But Martha's shoes were nearly worn through. Looking down at one of her sister's shoes, Caroline could even see a hole in the exact place where Martha's big toe would go. She knew it wasn't very nice, but she was glad that at least her shoes were nicer than Martha's.

Smoothing her yellow dress beneath her, Caroline sat down on the side of the bed and reached for her shoes. She tugged the shabby brown leather over her stockinged feet, and winced as she tried to push her toes and feet inside. Determined, she stood up and stamped her foot on the floor twice before her foot sank at last into the heel and her toes pressed up against the front of her shoe. Bending over, she tied the laces loosely above her foot and around her ankle. She did not want Mother to notice how small the shoes were. Since it was spring, she knew that she would have to wear them only for church, and she could bear the discomfort. Maybe she had to wear Martha's old dress, but she wasn't going to wear her holey old shoes, no matter what.

Caroline watched as Martha tried pulling on her pair of shoes. "I . . . can't . . . DO it!" Martha burst out as she dropped her foot and the shoe hanging halfway off it to the floor with a loud thump.

Mother continued tying Eliza's laces. "Yes, you *can* pull that shoe on, Martha, and you will.

Why, you wore them through the winter. That wasn't so long ago."

"They hurt, Mother!" Martha blurted out. "They don't fit!"

"They will fit long enough for us to go to church and return home. Now put on your shoes." Mother's voice was unbending. "Hurry, both of you, please."

"Yes, ma'am," Caroline answered as Mother descended the stairs with Eliza.

Cheeks flushed red and eyes flashing, Martha stood up from the bed and stamped her bare foot on the floor. "I'll go to church with no shoes at all, before I'll wear these awful shoes that don't even fit me," she muttered.

Caroline's mouth dropped open, and she spoke to Martha for the first time all day. "Even you wouldn't think of going to church without any shoes, Martha. Mother will never let you!"

"I run around outside all day long with no shoes!" Martha whispered fiercely, her eyes challenging Caroline.

Caroline still looked shocked. Martha threw

her hands up in the air and said, "Here! I'll show you!" Her face turned red as she finally pulled and stomped her shoe onto her foot. "Look at that, Caroline! You can see my toe right through this shoe!"

Caroline looked down at Martha's foot. For the first time all day, she felt like giggling. Sitting alone on the floor, Martha's shoes looked old and terrible. But with her big toe poking out of the tip, they looked terribly funny, too.

"I won't wear them," Martha announced. "Not to church. Not with this dress. And if Mother makes me wear them, I just won't go."

"Yes, you will, Martha." The girls turned to see Mother looking over the railing, and they caught their breath. "Your hem is a bit longer than usual, so no one will notice your shoes. As soon as I can get you another pair of shoes, I will. But you won't have them in time to wear to church this morning, so tie your laces and come downstairs. Now."

Martha opened her mouth to protest, but a quick warning glance from Mother helped her hold her tongue. Caroline waited until Martha finished lacing her shoes then followed Martha's flowing blue skirt down the stairs. "I'll take these horrid shoes off the first chance I get," Martha whispered over her shoulder to Caroline.

Her own toes already felt sore and cramped, but Caroline forced all thoughts of shoes and dresses out of her mind. Now she only hoped that Martha would not do anything terrible in church.

Cold Feet

Mother opened the kitchen door. Caroline could immediately feel and smell the fresh, cool air as a gust of it blew into the house. "It's a lovely spring day, so I don't think you need to wear your shawls, girls," Mother decided. "But you should carry them along just in case you get cold."

Caroline tucked her shawl under her arm, waved good-bye to Grandma and Thomas, and hurried out behind Mother and Martha to the Carpenters' wagon. Joseph and Henry were standing in the back of the wagon with Charlie Carpenter. Charlie was younger than Joseph and older than Henry, but much taller than both of them. His straight black hair was always falling into his dark eyes, and his grin never left his round, handsome face.

As Martha and Caroline approached the wagon, Charlie was waving his arms and shaking his head back and forth, talking and gesturing with great animation. Charlie always told the funniest stories, and this morning it seemed that even the birds had waited to begin their morning chorus just so they could listen to him. Caroline wished she could hear what he was saying, too, but all she could hear was Henry's loud laughter.

"Morning, ladies!" Mr. Carpenter jumped down over the high wide wagon wheel and thumped on the ground in front of Martha and Caroline. "Well, I never saw such pleasing church dresses!" he exclaimed. "You're going to be the prettiest girls sitting before the Lord today. No mistaking it."

"May I sit in back, please?" Martha asked, her face glowing.

"That's right where you'll have to sit, Miss

Martha, because your mother and littlest sister will be sitting up front with me and the Missus." Mr. Carpenter answered. He looked back at the wagon and called out, "Boys! Stop chattering like chipmunks, and help me get these young ladies into the wagon."

Joseph stepped over to the side of the wagon and reached down to Martha and Caroline. "Grab hold, Martha," he called.

"I can wait," Martha offered. "Take Caroline first."

Caroline reached up for Joseph's hand. She stepped onto the top of the wheel and over the side of the wooden wagon, holding her dress close to her legs so that it wouldn't get caught on any splinters. "Come sit over here, little Brownbraid," Henry called out, patting the empty bench beside him.

As Caroline placed her shawl on the seat beside her, she saw Charlie reach down for Martha's hand. "I'll help you, Martha," he said.

"Thank you." Martha reached up to take Charlie's hand.

"Careful now." Mr. Carpenter assisted her. "You don't want to tear such a pretty dress."

Caroline held her breath and watched her sister. She half expected Martha to rip or smudge the beautiful blue dress, but Martha stepped right up onto the wagon wheel and into the cart. Smoothing the soft material around her waist, she walked over to the bench and sat across from Caroline, right between Joseph and Charlie.

"I expect you'll act like gentlemen back here, boys. Remember, there are ladies in the wagon." Mr. Carpenter winked and lightly pounded the side of the wagon with his fist. Then he turned and helped Eliza and Mother up onto the bench in the front of the wagon, where Mrs. Carpenter sat waiting.

"Whew! We found enough seats for everyone," Mr. Carpenter called out. "Let's get to church!" The oxen snorted and jerked their thick brown heads as he walked around the wagon and gave each of them a quick pat on its hard, massive back. He climbed up into the front of the wagon, made a loud clicking noise, and shook loose the reins that hung around the oxen's necks. "Move along, old boys," he commanded.

Caroline gripped the edge of the bench as the oxen jerked the wagon and abruptly began their walk to church. She lifted her face toward the clear sky and took a deep breath of the cool spring air. The sun felt wonderful as it warmed her cheeks.

The oxen trudged down the dirt road on their way to town, and Caroline looked all around her. Every bit of earth not occupied by trees or houses or barns was dotted with clusters of fresh spring flowers. Fields of marsh marigolds heralded the spring, their brilliant yellow petals making the sunshine seem even brighter. The wild cherry trees celebrated too, all dressed up in their finest pale pink-and-white blossoms. Yellow buttons held together the trilliums' white oval petals and made them appear as though they had been kissed by sunshine. The sweet, new smell of flowers and grass blew through the air with the soft April wind. Springtime was here to stay.

"We must tell Mother that you'll be needing new shoes, Martha." Joseph's voice abruptly brought Caroline's attention back to the wagon, and Martha. "When you climbed up on the wagon wheel, I saw your toe had come clear through the leather."

Everyone in the back of the wagon looked down at Martha's feet, but they didn't see any shoes. Martha had already tucked her toes beneath the hem of her new blue dress.

"Hush, Joseph!" Martha glared at her brother. "I can't help if my shoes are old and worn out!"

"Well, your dress is the prettiest dress I ever saw, Martha," Charlie broke in. "Who cares about shoes, anyway?"

"I do," Caroline wanted to cry out as Martha's face lit up. "I care about shoes and dresses, much more than she does." But instead of saying anything, Caroline sat quietly and almost hoped that Joseph would say something awful to her sister again.

"Thank you, Charlie," Martha said, and folded her hands on her lap.

Charlie nodded and began to tell another story as the wagon creaked along to the very end of town. In no time at all, Mr. Carpenter stopped the oxen at the bottom of the grassy hill that led to the church. Caroline quickly forgot about dresses and shoes, and her heart swelled with pride as she gazed up at the freshly painted white church. It sat right on top of the hill, its pointed steeple nudging the heavens. The colored glass in the church's tall, narrow windows sparkled red and green, blue and gold in the sunshine. Caroline especially loved those windows because Father had selected them and helped place them in the church. The summer before he had gone away on the schooner, Father and Mr. Carpenter had worked with some of the townsfolk to build this little church. Until then, every churchgoer in town had attended Sunday services in the old log schoolhouse. For days and days Father and his friends had cleared the land, chopped wood, hammered, and sawed from the moment the sky began to brighten in the morning until just after all traces of light flickered out of it at night.

Caroline remembered how tired Father had been when he came home from building the church every night. "We're almost ready to let the Lord in, Charlotte," he'd say to Mother as he dropped his sore hands into the warm water of the washbasin and gently washed them. "Maybe tomorrow or the day after."

When the men finally finished pounding the last nail, Mother, Mrs. Carpenter, and all the ladies in town baked loaves and loaves of bread and cooked a big meal that all the children helped carry to the church. Right there, on the grass in front of their new church, the Quiners and their neighbors ate supper, sang hymns, and danced until bedtime. It was one of the happiest days that Caroline could remember.

"I'll jump out first and help the girls," Joseph was saying as Caroline stood up. "Charlie, give them a hand when they step onto the wagon wheel. Henry, go help Mother and Eliza, will you?"

"Yes, sir!" Henry teased. He grabbed the side of the wagon with both hands and swung his legs over the side.

Following Henry over the side of the wagon, Joseph steadied himself and reached for Martha's hand. Martha, holding on to Charlie's arm for support, climbed onto the wagon wheel and down into Joseph's waiting arms.

"Your turn, little Brownbraid." Caroline reached up to take Charlie's hand and was just about to step up onto the wagon wheel when she realized that she had left her shawl on the bench.

"Oh, Charlie," she said as she dropped his hand and turned back toward her seat, "I forgot my shawl." Reaching down, she took her shawl off the bench and went to tuck it under her arm. But one long strand from a corner of the shawl was wrapped around a piece of wood sticking out from the bench. "Oh no," she said, "my shawl is stuck."

"Can I help?" Charlie asked.

"I can do it," Caroline answered. She knelt on the floor of the wagon and began untangling the strip of yarn that had fastened itself to the jutting wood. As the shawl came free, Caroline spied something beneath the bench. For a moment, she thought it might be Martha's shawl, but when she reached down to get it, her fingers brushed soft and scratchy leather. Crouching down even lower, Caroline looked beneath the bench. The big hole in one of Martha's shoes was staring straight out at her.

"Are you certain you don't need help, Caroline?" Charlie asked from above.

Caroline's knees felt like they were stuck to the wagon. If Mother saw Martha in church without any shoes, Martha would be in trouble for a long, long time. Wondering if she should hide the shoes beneath her shawl and bring them to Martha, Caroline straightened up and looked over at her sister. Martha was smoothing the soft folds of her beautiful dress as she waited with Henry and Joseph.

Caroline glanced down at her faded yellow dress. If Martha didn't want to wear her shoes into church, then Caroline wasn't going to bring them to her.

Once everyone had gathered beside the wagon, the Quiners and the Carpenters walked up the short hill leading to the front door of the church. Caroline closely watched the hem of Martha's dress as they climbed through the grass. Martha was taking tiny steps so that her dress would cover her bare feet, and Mother and Mrs. Carpenter were so involved in their conversation that Mother never noticed the few times that a bare heel or toe peeked out from beneath Martha's dress.

The service had not yet begun inside the little church, so many of the churchgoers were standing out front, greeting each other with hugs, handshakes, and tales of the long winter just past. Mother spoke to some of the neighbors, while Joseph, Henry, and Charlie greeted friends from school. Martha, Caroline, and Eliza stood together, watching mothers and fathers and children milling around in their Sunday best.

On one side of the church, a stocky, beardless man with a head full of brown curls stood holding his daughter's hand. Caroline didn't remember ever seeing them in town before. The girl, who had even more brown curls than her father, was quietly watching all the people

around her, and she smiled when her eyes met
Caroline's.

There were six or seven other girls in the
churchyard. Most of them looked older than
Caroline, but one or two seemed to be about
her age. Caroline noticed every detail of their
dresses, their hair ribbons, and their shoes. She
wondered if any of them had to wear their sisters' old church dresses. Certainly the two tall,
pretty girls standing near the front of the
church did not. They both wore dresses
printed with tiny flowers, white stockings, and
new black shoes that were so shiny, they
reflected the glare of the sun. Their ribbons
matched their dresses as perfectly as their
white gloves matched the lace adorning their
necks and sleeves and hem.

"Let's go into church now, children,"
Mother said from behind Caroline. "Where did
your brothers run off to?"

"I'll go find them, Mother," Martha offered.
Without waiting for Mother's reply, she lifted
the hem of her blue silk dress and ran off
through the soft grass.

Caroline heard Mother gasp, but didn't stop looking at Martha long enough to see Mother's face. "She's not wearing any shoes," Caroline heard Mother whisper in disbelief. "Martha has gone and taken off her shoes!"

The girls with the white gloves who were standing near the front of the church heard Mother gasp, and turned to see Martha bounding down the hill. Instead of friendly chatter, Caroline now heard whispers, snickers, and laughter as they watched the girl with the beautiful blue dress running barefoot down the hill.

By the time Martha returned with Joseph, Henry, and Charlie, the two girls were looking straight at her. Fists clenched, Caroline stared at the girls as they pointed at Martha's feet and giggled softly into their gloved hands.

Joseph, Henry, and Charlie were laughing and joking with each other, and didn't notice Mother's face, Caroline's face, or the two girls who were giggling and pointing. But Martha noticed. The smile that had glowed on her face all morning quickly turned to surprise and then horror. She looked down at her bare feet and dropped the folds of material she had gathered in her hands so her lovely dress wouldn't be soiled by the grass and dirt.

Looking up at Mother, Caroline pleaded, "Let me go and get Martha's shoes, Mother. They're beneath the bench in the wagon."

"You'll do nothing of the sort, Caroline," Mother said firmly. "Wait here with Eliza." Mother marched over to Martha. Caroline watched her sister's fearful face and swallowed hard as Mother spoke to Joseph and then took Martha's arm and led her to the wagon. All around Caroline, people began filing into the church as Joseph jumped into the wagon, recovered Martha's shoes, and handed them to her.

Holding Eliza's hand tightly, Caroline listened to Martha's protests from down below. "I will not go to be made fun of! I will not go!" Martha was crying. But Mother wasn't listening. She stood above Martha and watched sternly as Martha pulled her shoes on.

By the time Mother, Martha and Joseph

started walking back up the hill, almost everyone was inside the church. The two girls with the white gloves were at the end of the line, talking loudly to each other, and Caroline cringed as she heard one of them say, "Mother says they live in town, but they must be poor, wild country girls. Who else would run barefoot after boys and wear a dress to church with no shoes?"

Without thinking, Caroline reached out and tugged on the dress of the girl nearest to her. "She's not a poor country girl!" Caroline said fiercely. "She's every bit as good as you, and looks prettier in her blue dress than you'll ever look in *any* dress!" Grabbing Eliza's hand again, Caroline turned her back on the girls before she even had a chance to see their shocked faces. She stood her ground as Mother, Joseph, and Martha finally joined them, and they silently walked into the church together.

Caroline didn't find any comfort looking up at the round stained-glass window that was set like a crown above the altar. When every voice in the church joined in the chorus of the first hymn, Caroline didn't feel at all like singing. Even the soft light of the lanterns that hung from the wooden beams high above her didn't bring her the peace that she always felt in this little church that Father had helped build. She sat on the hard wooden bench beside her sister and watched Martha's tears drop from her lowered face down to her lap.

Martha's new blue dress was soon stained with tears, but Caroline didn't think anything of it. She reached out, took Martha's hand, and squeezed as hard as she could.

Questions

Martha was in a terrible hurry to leave church. She followed Mother and her brothers and sisters to the door, where they waited for their turn to greet Reverend Fellows. The very moment that Mother finished her brief conversation with the pastor, Martha was out the door ahead of everyone. As she ran down the hill to the wagon, the wide stitches that held her shoe together split open in front, and all five toes burst out of the old leather.

"It seems you won't be wearing those shoes to church or anywhere after all, Martha,"

Mother said when she arrived at the wagon and looked down at the half-bare foot and torn shoe that her oldest daughter held up for her inspection. "You may take them off when we get home."

Caroline climbed up into the wagon, sat beside Martha, and looked down at her feet. The strip of leather that used to cover Martha's toes flapped up and down every time she moved her foot. Just watching all the flapping made Caroline's heart sink, because someday soon she knew that Mother would take her to the cobbler and have Martha's terrible shoes restitched so that Caroline could wear them. Curling her sore toes back inside her own worn shoes, Caroline willed her feet not to grow so fast.

On the way home, Mr. Carpenter and Charlie told stories, but Caroline hardly listened. She couldn't wait to get home and forget all about that awful morning. Martha pulled her shoes off the moment she stepped down from the wagon, and she turned to run into the house. Mother's "Just a minute,

Martha," stopped her bare feet in their tracks.

Walking back to the house a few steps behind her sisters and Mother, Caroline listened to Mother scold Martha again for taking her shoes off before church. Martha walked slowly and looked down at the ground as Mother spoke. "I'm afraid we will not be able to have the shoemaker make a new pair of shoes for you anytime soon, either. With all the laborers coming to Brookfield this spring to work the fields and build up the town, I have been mending a pair of trousers or making a new shirt every day. Seems I'm every bit as busy now as I ever was when I had my dress shop in Boston, and I need to spend every extra penny on sewing materials. New shoes will just have to wait until the weather turns cold and we have some pennies saved, Martha. You'll have to stay home and mind Thomas while the rest of us go to church on Sundays."

Caroline watched out of the corner of her eye as Martha looked up and a smile spread across her face.

But Mother wasn't finished. "All that being

said," she continued, "until you get a new pair of shoes and return to Sunday services with the rest of the family, Martha, you will spend your Sunday afternoons learning Bible lessons. Inside."

Caroline felt much better when Martha's smile disappeared. As sorry as she had felt for Martha in church that morning, she was glad that her sister would have to spend just as much time learning Bible lessons on Sunday afternoons as she had to spend sitting in church Sunday mornings.

For more than a month of Sundays, Martha stayed home with Thomas and spent her afternoons grumbling over her Bible studies instead of playing outside. And it wasn't until the evening before their first day of school, six weeks after she first wore her new blue dress to church, that Martha spoke to Caroline about that terrible morning.

Mother insisted that Caroline and Martha go to bed right after supper. "You will need to be up at the first light of day tomorrow," she said.

"You musn't be late for your first day of school."

Caroline wondered if there was anything left to do that could make them late for school. Mother had already helped with their baths and made certain that every last inch of their skin was scrubbed clean. Their hair was freshly washed, dried, and brushed. All they had to do in the morning was pull on their petticoats and dresses, and have Grandma braid their hair. They could do that in no time.

As soon as Caroline, Martha, and Eliza had tied the strings of their nightcaps and climbed into bed, Mother tucked them in and listened to their prayers. "Good night, dear girls," she said as she kissed their foreheads one by one.

Caroline and Eliza murmured their good-nights, and Martha suddenly burst out, "Oh Mother, must we go to school tomorrow?"

The evening darkness had only just begun to settle over the room, so Caroline could clearly see the surprise in Mother's eyes as she turned back to Martha. "Why just a few short months ago, you could hardly sit still for wanting to go to school," she said.

"That's only because Henry and Joseph were going, too," Martha replied honestly. "Why don't they have to go to school tomorrow?"

Mother sat down beside Martha on the edge of the bed. "I've explained this to you before, Martha. Many children in Brookfield need schooling, and it is simply not possible to fit all of you together in that little schoolhouse. So now that it's summer, and most boys are needed to work the fields, they won't be going to school. There's only room enough in the school for the littlest boys who can't do the hard work just yet, and young ladies like you and Caroline."

"I could work hard outside, too," Martha said.

"When you return from school each day, Martha, you may work outside as hard as you like," Mother answered.

"When are Henry and Joseph going to bed, Mother?" Martha asked so quietly that Caroline wondered if she really wanted Mother to hear her question.

"As soon as I tell them to do so, Martha." The edge in Mother's voice clearly suggested that Martha should not ask any more questions. "To sleep, now. All of you."

Waiting until she heard the last of Mother's footsteps echo on the wooden stairs below, Martha whispered, "Are you scared, Caroline?"

"About what?" Caroline whispered back.

"About going to school tomorrow."

"I don't think so," Caroline said slowly.

"Well, you should be."

"But why, Martha?" Caroline asked, even though she wasn't at all certain that she wanted to know.

"That old Mr. Henderson is the new schoolmaster, and he is nothing like the lady who taught lessons last summer. Folks say he is awful. He asks all sorts of questions that no one knows the answers to, and all the other students laugh if you tell him the wrong answer. And"—Martha's voice was now raised above a whisper—"if you make the littlest noise, even if you just cough or sneeze, the schoolmaster makes you come right up to the front of the

room, and then he takes a big wooden stick
out of his desk and hits you hard as he can on
the knuckles, right in front of all the other
kids! Leaves your fingers smarting for a whole
week!"

"That's not true!" Caroline almost cried
out in disbelief. She had heard about Mr.
Henderson on the day they made the wagon
pie, but Joseph and Henry hadn't said a word
about him being so terrible.

"Is so true." Martha's nightcapped head
nodded up and down. "I know, Caroline, 'cause
I heard Henry and Joseph telling stories about
him themselves."

Caroline was so surprised, she couldn't
speak. The room was silent until Martha
added, "I just hope we don't see those dreadful
girls again."

Looking past Eliza, who was now fast
asleep, Caroline whispered, "What girls?"

"Remember the last time I went to church
with you and my shoe fell apart? Remember
those girls who wore the white gloves and the
lacy dresses? Those girls who wouldn't stop

pointing at my feet and laughing? I never saw them before that morning, and I hope all the way to heaven that they won't be at school."

Caroline remembered the girls so clearly, it was as though they were standing right in front of her. She pictured their gloves, their flowered print dresses trimmed with white lace, the heels and buckles on their brand-new black shoes, the bright, colorful ribbons that matched their dresses, and their mocking faces. Her cheeks grew hot with shame and anger as she remembered yelling at them, and Caroline was most thankful that Mother had not witnessed her outburst.

"I hope we don't *ever* see them again, Martha," Caroline said firmly. Then she sighed softly.

"Me, too." Martha turned over beneath the sheet and settled with her back to Caroline and Eliza. "G'night, Caroline."

"Night."

The soft breeze that fluttered in through the bedroom window was warmer than usual for an evening so early in June, so Caroline pushed the sheet down from her shoulders to her waist. Lying still, she stared up at the dark ceiling beams above her head and listened to the soft chatter of the voices in the room below. Joseph and Henry were still playing checkers. Mother and Grandma were working together at the sewing table, as they did most evenings. For a moment, Caroline longed to be sitting with them, feeling happy and safe. Mother always said that school was interesting and fun. If only Mother could go with them to school tomorrow, too.

Closing her eyes, Caroline listened to her sisters now breathing softly beside her and thought about school. Day after day that winter she had wished she could go to school with Henry and Joseph. She couldn't wait to have her own reader and learn all about spelling and reading and adding up numbers. But Henry and Joseph had never told her about the terrible schoolmaster. Her stomach flip-flopped at the very thought of him. What questions would he ask? Would all the other children know much more than she did? Would they laugh at her? And what if she couldn't stop her sneezes or coughs?

Trying to think about anything but school, Caroline looked up into the darkness, and her thoughts wandered back to those girls she had seen at church. If they were in the schoolhouse tomorrow, they would certainly have new dresses. They might even wear their white gloves and the shiny black shoes with the fancy heels. Caroline never wore shoes in the summer unless she was going to church. And even though Mother had scrubbed her everyday dress clean for her first day of school, the light-blue cotton was still old and faded, and the dress was too short for her now. Caroline desperately wished that Mother would make her a new dress. But Mother was so busy with her sewing and mending for other people, she didn't have time to make any new dresses for little girls. And Caroline's light-blue dress, short as it was, was better than any other old dress of Martha's that Mother might mend and hem for her.

" 'Pride goeth before destruction, and an

haughty spirit before a fall.'" Mother always quoted that verse when one of her children complained about wearing old clothes or worn shoes. Caroline wasn't certain what it meant. But in the silent darkness she could almost hear Mother saying it to her now, just as if she were sitting beside Caroline listening to her thoughts.

Shifting her head on the pillow one last time, Caroline shut her eyes tightly and tried to imagine what a brand-new reader might look like. Her image of clean white pages filled with letters and words was soon replaced by one of a large, angry man holding a long wooden stick in his pudgy hand. He was dressed in black from his tie to his boots. The sagging cheeks on the man's heavy face drooped over his chin, and his furry black eyebrows scrunched together as he frowned and called out, "Caroline Quiner! That answer is incorrect!" Flinging the stick up into the air, he brought it down in a wide arc and crashed it on the table. At the very same instant, two pretty girls seated beside him, wearing white gloves, burst into a fit of giggles.

Caroline's eyelids flew open, and she sat straight up in bed. The darkness did not comfort her, nor did the soft sounds of slumber in the bed beside her or the chatter in the room below. Pulling the sheet all the way up to her chin, she eased herself slowly back down on the mattress and stared straight up at the ceiling. Never before had she dreaded anything quite so much as going to school.

School

When Mother peered through the stair railing early the next morning, Caroline was not yet awake. Mother climbed the last few stairs into the room, stood over the bed, and gently touched Caroline's and Martha's cheeks.

"Wake up now, girls," she said softly. "You must rise quickly. The schoolmaster won't wait for sleepy-eyed children."

Caroline opened her eyes the moment Mother said the dreaded word. But instead of seeing bushy eyebrows and sagging cheeks, she found Mother's green eyes smiling down at her.

"Good morning, Mother," Caroline said.

"I thought you might just sleep the day away." Mother's voice was full of worry. "Are you not feeling well, Caroline? I cannot remember a morning past when I didn't find you wide awake and waiting for me as I climbed the stairs."

Caroline longed to tell Mother about the terrible dreams that had kept her tossing in her sleep all night. For a moment she even thought she might tell Mother she felt sick. Her stomach *was* full of flutters, after all. Perhaps Mother might let her stay away from the schoolhouse for a day or two.

"You've been waiting and waiting for your first day of school, Caroline," Mother said, "and you don't appear to be ill. Whatever is wrong?"

Looking up at Mother, Caroline noticed that her bright green eyes had dark circles beneath them. Caroline was certain that she had been mending and sewing well into the night. With all that Mother had to worry about, Caroline didn't have their heart to tell her she felt sick and worry her even more.

"I'm fine." Caroline looked away from Mother's eyes. "I feel tired, is all."

"A warm breakfast will surely cure that." Mother stood up. "Now hurry and dress, girls. There is still plenty to do before you get on your way to school."

"Are Joseph and Henry going to help?" Martha looked toward the center of the room, but she didn't see any movement or hear any noises behind the curtain.

"Henry and Joseph left the house before the break of day to help Mr. Carpenter and Charlie repair the side of their barn. They made such a clatter running down the stairs, I'm surprised you didn't hear them!" Mother exclaimed. "Now that's more than enough chatter for one morning, girls. I expect to see you downstairs the moment your dresses are buttoned. I won't have you be late for your first day of school."

"Yes, ma'am," Caroline and Martha answered, jumping out of bed.

"Eliza go, too!" Eliza called to Mother, her big round eyes hopeful.

"Oh no, Eliza." Mother patted her golden

curls. "You must stay here and help Grandma and me make dinner and watch Thomas. Don't worry, little one. Your sisters will be home from school in no time."

As Caroline got dressed, she wished that she and Martha were already walking home. Pulling her light-blue dress over her petticoats, Caroline remembered that Mother had told them not to wear their aprons to school. She looked down at her blue dress and longed to wear her apron, if only to hide the faded fabric and the tiny stains that never went away no matter how hard Mother scrubbed them on wash day. Her dress was also too short. Caroline pulled at her hem and sleeves, thinking she just might be able to stretch them a little, but it was no use. Picking up her ribbon, she trudged downstairs.

"Mother says you're not yourself today," Grandma whispered in her ear as she pulled and twisted the three thick sections of Caroline's brown hair into a braid. "Can Grandma help?"

Looking up into Grandma's kind eyes, Caroline decided that it would be safe to tell Grandma about her dreams and Martha's story.

But just as she was about to speak, Martha interrupted.

"She's afraid to go to school, Grandma," Martha said matter-of-factly. "She's afraid of the schoolmaster."

"Is that true, dear?" Grandma asked quietly as she tied Caroline's ribbon in a bow around the bottom of her braid.

"Martha's the one who's afraid, Grandma." Caroline flashed a warning look at her older sister. "She's the one who told me about the awful schoolmaster!"

"I am not afraid!" Martha shot back at Caroline, and stamped her foot. "I've already been to school for one whole summer, and no silly schoolmaster will ever scare me!"

"Martha!" Grandma's voice rose in surprise as Caroline and Martha stood and stared at each other.

"What is all this commotion about?" Mother walked swiftly across the room, holding Thomas in her arms.

"Caroline says I'm afraid, Mother, but it's not true!"

"Afraid of what?" Mother asked calmly.

"Afraid to go to school. Afraid of the school-master," Martha continued. "Imagine! Me, afraid! Why, I'm not afraid of *anything*!"

Mother looked at Caroline. "What makes you think that your sister is afraid of the schoolmaster, Caroline?"

"She said *I* should be afraid, Mother." Caroline's voice quivered, but she did not cry. No matter what, she would not cry in front of Martha. "She said the schoolmaster raps your knuckles if you cough or sneeze. Then she told Grandma that I was afraid to go to school."

"Why, that's just plain silliness, Caroline," Mother said. Looking down at Caroline, her eyes were now full of understanding. "If you are a good girl in school, as I am certain you will be, the schoolmaster will not find any need to discipline you. The schoolmaster will teach you to read and to spell. Anything you imagine beyond that is utter nonsense. Now let Grandma finish your braids, girls. Your breakfast is getting cold, and you must soon be on your way."

Martha stood silently as Grandma finished tying her ribbons into bows on the ends of her braids. The girls were silent as they ate their corn bread and mush. They were even silent as they washed and dried the breakfast dishes and stacked them on the dish dresser.

Standing in the kitchen doorway while Mother adjusted their bows, straightened their dresses, and tied their sunbonnets, they still did not speak.

As soon as she finished, Mother looked Caroline and Martha over one last time and said, "How pretty you both look for your first day of school. Now remember, you will have plenty of time to walk home from the schoolhouse and have dinner at home this noon. Joseph and Henry rarely had the time during the winter, with all the snow and bitter winds, but in this lovely warm weather, the walk will be a pleasure."

Kneeling down in front of Caroline, Mother looked at her very seriously. "This is one of the most important things you will ever do, Caroline, going to school. Be a good girl and study hard." Turning to Martha, Mother added, "I expect the same from you, Martha. And remember, the schoolmaster always knows what is best."

"Yes, ma'am," Martha and Caroline answered solemnly.

Caroline's heart was pounding as they left the house. After they had walked a short distance, Martha spoke first. "Mother knows the schoolmaster is every bit as terrible as I said, Caroline, or she never would have told me that he always knows best. Besides, I heard Joseph and Henry say so, and they don't make up such stories."

Walking beside the bumpy, dirt road through a field of grass that was still cool and damp with morning dew, Caroline did not answer. The warm sun climbing through slivers of clouds and a morning chorus of cardinals usually cheered her, but they could not today. Her stomach was all fluttery again. Her eyes and head ached. And she was still mad at Martha.

Soggy blades of grass and tiny clumps of dirt

clung to Caroline's bare feet, and every now and again she stopped to brush them off before continuing on her way. She was in no hurry to get to the schoolhouse, and Martha was soon far ahead of her.

Turning to find Caroline quite a distance behind, Martha shouted in the loud voice that Mother always hushed, "You'd best hurry, Caroline Lake Quiner, or you'll get a caning just for being late on the very first day of school!"

The possibility of a caning startled Caroline. It had never occured to her that the schoolmaster might hit her fingers simply because she arrived late at the schoolhouse. Lifting the hem of her skirt above the damp grass, she ran as fast as she could, paying no attention to anything that stuck to her feet.

"Oh, Martha, we must run!" Caroline puffed quick, hurried breaths as she caught up to Martha. "We must run all the way to the schoolhouse."

"If you would just keep walking without stopping all the time, we'll arrive at the schoolhouse with plenty of minutes to spare, and the schoolmaster won't have any reason to be angry." Martha looked down at her little sister, her brown eyes flashing. "And don't think you can go ahead without me. I know the way better than you do."

"You *are* frightened of him!" Caroline turned to her big sister, her eyes wide with surprise.

"Only a little," Martha admitted grudgingly. "I mostly think we should be on time for our first day of school, is all."

As they stood on the edge of town, Martha reached out for Caroline's hand and held it tightly. Together they walked past the crowd of townsfolk who had congregated in front of the grocer's stoop. They hurried by one of the noisy taverns, the wagonmaker's shop, and the blacksmith shop, where the smith stood outside the front door, deep in conversation with one of the shoemakers in town. Tipping his hat to Martha and Caroline, the blacksmith called out, "Good day to you, young ladies!"

"Good morning, Mr. Stam." Martha waved.

Caroline scarcely noticed people passing,

horses clomping, or laborers pounding nails and chopping wood all around her on the busy street. All she could think about was arriving at school. On time.

At the far end of town, Caroline and Martha crossed a narrow field that led to a steep hill. Hurrying up the hill, they found themselves in a large meadow, which was edged with forests. The warm early-summer breeze stirred the grass and wildflowers, bending them over, then quickly straightening them up. Her skirt flapping with the wildflowers, Caroline stopped and looked at the schoolhouse, which was now only a short walk away.

The schoolhouse looked very much like any frame house in town, though in front there was only one tall, narrow door and no windows at all. The sun glinted off the five glass windows that were all in a row on one side of the schoolhouse. Caroline hoped that she could sit near one of the windows.

The meadow in front of the schoolhouse sparkled as every color of wildflower mixed with the reds and yellows, blues and whites of schoolgirls' dresses. Caroline had never before seen so many girls her age in one place; talking with each other, playing, or simply waiting to begin their first day of school. A small crowd of little boys in trousers, shirts, and suspenders scampered about the field, too, running races, making silly faces, or pulling the braids of their unsuspecting sisters.

"We won't hear very much if we try to listen to the schoolmaster from all the way back here," Martha remarked. "Let's go, Caroline."

Caroline could tell that Martha wasn't teasing. Martha sounded worried—scared, even. Together they hurried along until they were standing in the tall grass among the other children.

"There they are," Martha whispered.

"Who?" Caroline asked.

"Those girls with the white gloves."

Martha did not need to answer. Caroline had already seen the girls. They were standing together beneath a maple tree whose leafy branches curved, dipped and turned every which way. Both girls wore new cotton dresses.

One girl's yellow dress had tiny red flowers printed all over its skirt. The other girl's pink dress had little blue dots covering it from neckline to hem. The soft cotton dresses flowed down to the girls' ankles and met the same shiny black heeled shoes they had worn to church weeks ago. Their ribbons again matched their dresses, though they didn't wear their white gloves. Caroline thought they looked perfectly, awfully wonderful.

"I'll be right back, Caroline," Martha said determinedly.

"Wait, Martha!" Caroline called out after her. "You mustn't cause any trouble!"

Martha marched across the meadow without paying any attention to the young boys scurrying around her. Her bonnet fell down past her shoulders, keeping her braids from swinging back and forth as she took long strides. Stepping in front of the girls, she folded her arms in front of her. She was just about to speak when Caroline ran up behind her.

"See! I'm not wearing any shoes today, either." Martha held out her bare foot, and much to Caroline's surprise, kept her voice low. "And every single day for the rest of this summer, I won't wear any shoes. Even if I had a pair as bright and shiny as yours, I wouldn't wear them. My brother says that feet just want to roam free in the summertime, and it seems to me that folks shouldn't have to wear shoes that pinch their toes and make their heels all sore and blistered. So if you don't like my dress, or my shoes, whether I'm wearing them or not, I say keep your words to yourself."

"Let's go now, Martha," Caroline whispered urgently.

Martha's braids broke free from the bonnet that restrained them as she turned away from the girls and their shocked faces. "Let's go wait on the other side of the field for the schoolmaster to ring the bell, Caroline," she said proudly.

Caroline and Martha crossed in front of the schoolhouse just as a young lady walked out the tall narrow door. She was wearing a gray dress with a full skirt and one row of little white buttons that started just beneath her chin and traveled all the way down to her waist. Her yellow hair was wound tightly in a bun high on her head, and her kind eyes were dark brown. As Caroline and Martha passed in front of her, the lady smiled at Caroline. Then she began ringing a high-pitched bell.

"That lady seems much nicer than those other girls, Martha," Caroline said as she looked back over her shoulder. "I wonder if she is their friend."

"Hush, Caroline." Martha stopped walking and said excitedly, "I think she is the schoolmistress. She must be an even newer teacher than the schoolmaster that Joseph and Henry had!"

"The schoolmistress! Why, she isn't much older-looking than Joseph!" Caroline cried, and clapped her hand over her mouth.

Martha, too, looked very, very surprised. "Only the schoolmistress rings the bell like that. It means we all have to go into the building now. Lessons are about to begin."

"But you said that the schoolmaster was a man! You said . . ."

"I only said what I heard Henry and Joseph say." Martha shrugged. "Let's go inside before there is no room left on the benches."

The schoolmistress nodded her head as Caroline and Martha walked past her on their way into the schoolhouse. "Good morning, young ladies," she said in a gentle but firm voice.

Rows of benches filled the room from front to back, and Martha looked up and down them, searching for a place to sit.

"Please, Martha," Caroline whispered, "may we sit near the windows?"

"I think so." Martha quickly found empty seats on the side of the room where sunlight poured onto the benches and spilled to the plank floor.

After they were seated, Martha turned to look for some of the girls she'd met in the schoolhouse last summer. Caroline examined every detail of the room around her. A single wooden table was the only piece of furniture at the front of the room, and a black woodstove stood in the corner. In front of the benches, a slate board hung from the ceiling like a big black wall. Beside it hung a large picture of different colored shapes and a painting of a very serious looking man.

"Who's that, Martha?" Caroline asked, pointing to the portrait.

"It's President Polk." A girl's soft voice startled Caroline, and she edged backward on the hard wooden bench.

"I'm sorry. I didn't mean to surprise you. I was only hoping to find a seat by the window." Dark-brown curls fell softly over the girl's forehead from beneath the top of her bonnet, and her cheeks were round and pink. Her brown dress was faded but clean, and her feet were bare, just like Caroline's.

"Martha, move over some," Caroline said as she edged down the bench and made room.

The girl with the curls sat down beside Caroline and set a small tin pail on the floor at her feet. "My name is Anna," she whispered in Caroline's ear. "I saw you at church that day when your sister had so much trouble. Those girls had no right to laugh like they did. I heard what you said to them after your sister ran down the hill, and I also heard what your sister said to them today. I sure hope I can sit with both of you from now on."

As Anna finished speaking, the schoolmistress walked to the front of the room, and Caroline didn't have time to whisper a reply. The smile that lit her face was her answer, and Anna understood perfectly.

"Good morning." The young lady teacher greeted the class. "My name is Miss Morgan. Please sit quietly in your seats until I finish recording all your names."

Calling every new student up to her desk one by one, the schoolmistress penciled each name in a little gray book filled with blank pages. Then she asked each student to spell and read for her.

"Good morning, Miss Caroline Quiner," she said as Caroline stepped in front of her desk.

"Good morning, Miss Morgan."

"Have you learned any of your letters or numbers yet?"

Caroline's stomach was all fluttery as she

spoke, but her voice sounded very certain.

"Mother and Grandma have taught me to print most of the letters in the alphabet, and I've even stitched most every one on my sampler!"

"Well, that's just fine, Caroline," Miss Morgan praised. "Can you spell or read any words yet?"

"Only some small words, ma'am," Caroline answered, "but I know a whole page of Bible verses."

Handing Caroline a thin, gray book from the top of a stack of gray books, Miss Morgan said encouragingly, "Here's a primer to begin with, Caroline. I expect you'll be sharing your sister's reader and her speller by the Fourth of July."

"Oh please, how far away is that, ma'am?" Caroline asked eagerly.

"A month plus a day or two," she replied kindly.

"Thank you, ma'am," Caroline said, and headed back to her bench, where Anna and Martha were already seated and holding their new readers and spellers. She was just about to sit down when a girl sitting on the bench in front of her sneezed. Caroline shot a scared look at Martha. They waited, wondering if the schoolmistress would reach for her wooden stick.

Miss Morgan looked up from the student she was speaking to. "Bless you, Miss Dane," she said.

Caroline's stomach flutters disappeared as she sat down and opened her primer. Sunlight spilled onto the first clean, crisp page, and then the second, and Caroline soon realized that she knew all the letters and most of the words on the first four pages. By the time she turned to page five, the schoolmistress was announcing it was time for dinner.

Anna picked up her tin pail and walked out the door in front of Caroline and Martha. As they pulled their bonnets up over their heads in the hot sunshine, Caroline offered, "Anna, we can walk with you to your house and then come get you after dinner."

"I've brought my dinner along, thank you," Anna replied. "I plan to find a shady patch of grass and eat my lunch right here. I'll save our seats on the bench until you and Martha get back from dinner."

"Oh, no, Anna," Martha said. "Just bring your pail along home with us."

"Yes! Please!" Caroline cried. "You can meet Mother and Grandma, and Thomas, and Eliza. Maybe even Joseph and Henry will be there, if they've finished fixing Mr. Ben's barn!"

"All those folks live in one house?" Anna's bright blue eyes sparkled at the very thought.

"All but Mr. Ben." Martha laughed, adding, "We must call him Mr. Carpenter whenever Mother is in the room."

"It won't be too much trouble, then?"

Martha and Caroline answered by linking arms with Anna and marching off through the meadow of grass and wildflowers. They told stories as they walked arm in arm all the way through town, giggled as they crossed the grassy field by the dusty, dirt road, and whispered to each other happily as they hurried up to the kitchen door of the frame house.

In a Hurry

The table was already set with dishes, cups, forks, and spoons, and the steaming chicken pie, crusty bread, butter, and milk clustered in the center of the table made it look more than full.

"We can eat now, Mother!" Henry shouted as Caroline, Martha, and Anna burst through the kitchen door.

Caroline took a deep breath. All the delicious aromas in the room mixed with the musky smell of firewood burning in the hearth. For the first time all day, Caroline felt hungry.

"Henry Odin Quiner, you will not taste one

bite until everyone is seated at the table," Mother said sternly. "And then you will wait until everyone is served."

Turning toward the door, Mother noticed their guest for the first time.

"This is Anna, Mother," Caroline quickly explained when she saw the surprise in Mother's eyes. "We met at school this morning. She didn't have anyone to eat dinner with, so we brought her home to eat with us. She has her own dinner pail."

Mother smiled warmly. "Welcome, Anna. You may come eat dinner with us whenever you like. And you need not bring your dinner pail. We do not have much, but you certainly are welcome to share it."

"Thank you kindly, ma'am," Anna replied gratefully.

"Wash up quickly, girls," Mother said. "We must hurry and get you fed so that you can be back on your way to the schoolhouse."

Caroline caught up Anna's hand and pulled her over to the washstand. "We wash up over here, Anna," she explained.

Whispering and laughing, Caroline, Martha, and Anna took off their bonnets. They washed their faces and hands and wiped them dry.

"Come sit please," Henry called out from the table. "You're all slower than molasses in January."

"Henry Odin Quiner!" Mother flashed him another warning as the rest of the Quiners and Anna gathered and sat down at the table. They bowed their heads and prayed, and Mother began serving dinner. "How was your first morning at the schoolhouse, Caroline?" she asked as she spooned chicken pie onto each plate.

"Oh, Mother, it was so wonderful!" Caroline said exuberantly. "We don't have a schoolmaster. We have a schoolmistress, and her name is Miss Morgan. She is only a little bit older than Joseph, I think, and she wears a dress that has more buttons on it than all of our dresses put together!"

"And she didn't even hit anybody when they sneezed!" Martha added as she wrinkled her nose at Henry. "So there!"

"Well, goodness glory, Caroline," Mother

said. "It doesn't sound so awful, after all."

"No, ma'am," Caroline answered, biting into her steaming chicken pie. "I spelled some words for the teacher, and read as many as I knew how to read. Miss Morgan gave me my very own primer, and she said that it will help me learn to read and spell better. She even said that I might be able to share Martha's reader and speller by the Fourth of July! That's just one month, plus a day or two."

"It certainly sounds like you had a fine beginning, Caroline." Mother smiled.

"Yes, ma'am," Caroline answered proudly.

"Good thing Old Man, I mean, Mr. Henderson isn't giving lessons this summer," Henry said as he popped a piece of warm bread into his mouth.

"That will be quite enough, Henry-O. Shame on you for filling your sisters' heads with such nonsense. Break that bread into smaller pieces before you eat it, young man, and save some butter for everyone else at the table."

"I want butter!" piped up Eliza.

Joseph reached for the tub of butter from Henry, spread some on a small piece of bread, and handed it to his littlest sister. "Here, Eliza," he said.

"Thank you, Joseph," Mother said. "Chew slowly, Eliza." Turning to Anna, she then offered, "Would you like some bread and butter, Anna?"

"Why, yes, please." Anna smiled. "Thank you, ma'am."

"Please pass the butter to Anna, Joseph," Mother said, breaking off a warm piece of bread. "Take as much as you like, Anna. There's plenty to go around."

Mother turned and looked at Henry. His mouth was full of his last bite of pie. "You may have another piece of bread and butter after Anna is finished with it, Henry," she said.

"Thank you, ma'am," Henry mumbled. He held his empty plate up high and was just about to ask for another serving of chicken pie when Grandma quickly spooned some onto his plate.

"I was just about to offer second helpings,

Charlotte," Grandma said. "Is that all right with you?"

"It's fine, Mother Quiner," Mother replied, raising her eyebrows at Henry. "Thank you."

Henry happily took the butter from Anna and spread a thick covering of it all over his bread.

Mother watched him in amazement. "I didn't think it possible that anyone could eat more butter than your father, Henry-O, but you have proven me wrong." Turning to Anna, Mother explained, "Their father always ate as much butter as he could get his hands on."

Caroline and Martha looked at each other across the table, and Caroline could tell that Martha was thinking what she was thinking. Mother was talking about Father, and she wasn't answering a question or telling a story. She was talking about Father because she wanted to, and she didn't even look or sound sad. Martha's look from across the table told Caroline that she had noticed it as well.

"Have you finished helping Mr. Carpenter?" Mother asked Joseph.

"Yes, ma'am," Joseph replied. "His barn door wouldn't break now if all his hogs and oxen charged it at once."

"So, then, you and Henry will have time to tend the garden this afternoon?"

Joseph nodded. "We've already got a bunch of sprouts poking up in most every row. They already need to be separated, and the rest of the garden needs a good weeding. So far, everything we planted seems to have taken root."

"That's very good news, Joseph," Mother said. "When I finish mending one last shirt after dinner, I'll come see. We need to grow as much as we can this year, so no matter what storms the Lord may send us, we'll have enough food to carry us through the winter."

Caroline shivered as she remembered the long, hungry winter that had just passed. Picking up her bread and butter, she breathed in its good smell. Only a few months ago, Caroline had wished with all her heart that she could be smelling and eating warm, fresh bread and butter. Only a few months ago, their garden, now green and alive with the promise of a rich harvest, had been frozen and dead.

"Cup! Cup!" Thomas banged his spoon on his plate. Mother held a small tin cup to his lips and helped him sip his milk. Forks clanged against plates, and Grandma served yet another helping around the table.

As Caroline finished her last bite of chicken pie, she looked across the table at Anna. Her new friend's face glowed as she listened and watched all the flurry of activity around her. Anna smiled back brightly at Caroline as though they shared a special secret.

Just a few hours earlier, Caroline had sat at this very same table for breakfast. Her stomach had been tied in frightened knots as she thought about the terrible schoolmaster. Now, the early-summer sun was fixed at the top of the sky, and Caroline could not think of a single thing that made her angry or sad. She had a new friend, a brand-new primer, and a whole summer of new adventures ahead.

Caroline set her fork down on her empty plate. "May I begin clearing the dishes now, Mother?" she asked.

"My, but you are in a hurry, Caroline," Mother exclaimed.

Jumping up from the table, Caroline answered, "Yes, ma'am," and picked up her plate. She could not wait to get back outside and let the summer begin.